NUCLEAR FAMILY

*A Tragicomic Novel
in Letters*

SUSANNA FOGEL

A Holt Paperback
Henry Holt and Company   New York

Holt Paperbacks
Henry Holt and Company
Publishers since 1866
175 Fifth Avenue
New York, New York 10010
www.henryholt.com

Library of Congress Cataloging-in-Publication Data

Names: Fogel, Susanna, author.
Title: Nuclear family : a tragicomic novel in letters / Susanna Fogel.
Description: First edition. | New York : Henry Holt and Company, 2017.
Identifiers: LCCN 2016043920| ISBN 9781250165237 (paperback) | ISBN
    9781627797924 (electronic book)
Subjects: LCSH: Jewish families—Fiction. | Domestic fiction. | Epistolary
    fiction. | Jewish fiction. | Satire. | BISAC: HUMOR / Topic / Marriage &
    Family. | HUMOR / Topic / Relationships. | FICTION / Humorous.
Classification: LCC PS3606.O396 2017 | DDC 813/.6—dc23
LC record available at https://lccn.loc.gov/2016043920

Our books may be purchased in bulk for promotional, educational, or business use. Please contact your local bookseller or the Macmillan Corporate and Premium Sales Department at (800) 221-7945, extension 5442, or by e-mail at MacmillanSpecialMarkets@macmillan.com.

First Edition 2017

Designed by Meryl Sussman Levavi

Printed in the United States of America

1 3 5 7 9 10 8 6 4 2

NUCLEAR FAMILY

For my family—despite our many fractures and diasporas, we'll always be united by our ability to laugh at ourselves. No pressure.

Your Dad Is Less Than Thrilled about Your Childhood Dream

Dear Julie,

It sounds like you are enjoying summer camp in Maine. I have no doubt your chief concern in receiving this "care package" from your parents will be the bag of Starburst candies we have enclosed per your request. I'm sure you will also wax nostalgic at your mother's attached note detailing her progress with her tomato garden and how much your little sister has grown.

However, I ask that you also take a moment to consider this personal note I have included expressing some concern about the content of your last letter to us.

Specifically, you mention that you and a girl named "Mandy" intend to apply to the same university, an institution in Virginia that allows you to bring your own horse to campus. I would assume this is a two-year college. Suffice it to say, I question the academic rigor of any environment that advertises the accessibility of livestock as a chief amenity. You also mention a collective goal shared with Mandy and two other new acquaintances to move to Florida after graduation and open a stable you will name "Four Girls Farms."

I am seriously concerned about your academic and professional ambitions, or apparent lack thereof. Your mother requested I table this discussion for several years, but as I told her, my own summer after seventh grade, auditing physics courses at Caltech, was instrumental in my decision to pursue a career in medicine. All of which is to say: though the momentary pleasure of sailing over an obstacle on horseback may feel like an ascent, I encourage you to aspire to greater heights for yourself in life.

That said, as a neurologist, I was pleased to see in your last enclosed photo that you were wearing protective headgear.

Dad

Your Mom Wants to Reassure You That What She Just Caught You Doing Is Totally Natural

Hi sweetheart—
I hope I'm not embarrassing you by slipping this under your door. I didn't know if the reason you didn't come down to dinner is that you felt bad about what I saw earlier when I walked into your room with the laundry. I'm so sorry I didn't knock first. That was a violation of your privacy and as a therapist I should have known better. Just so you know, I didn't say anything to Dad at dinner. In the future, I will assume that every time your bedroom door is closed you are doing private things in there.

I also wanted to let you know that I noticed the picture of your cousin Paul nearby. I'm not sure if there was any connection, but if there was, that is also totally normal! Often, some of our first intimate feelings are inspired by members of our family. I remember when I was about your age, I had some very confusing feelings about my brother (Uncle Ken), who was a point guard on the Bronx Science basketball team and very handsome growing up. I can show you pictures sometime if you like.

I hope this letter makes you feel less embarrassed.

Love,
Mom

Your Dad Does Not Care to Negotiate with You about Hanukkah

Dear Julie,

I received your handwritten note in my office requesting that your mother and I supplant our traditional eight small gifts at Hanukkah with one "Super Nintendo" video game console, to be bestowed upon you the first night.

Unfortunately, as I told your mother, I do not think this is a sound investment for reasons having nothing to do with our religious beliefs. (After all, as even the most unobservant Jew may note, Hanukkah is in fact a third-tier holiday that has benefitted from a massive PR campaign here in the States due to its proximity to Christmas.) The fact of the matter is that I am well aware of current research studies in my field on the long-term effects of video games on brain chemistry. As their results are yet unproven, I would be as negligent in allowing my own daughter to be a test case for this potential mental erosion as I would in allowing her to ingest off-market SSRIs in Phase One clinical trials.

That said, I will happily factor in the spirit of your request when purchasing your gifts this holiday season. I've asked my research assistant to cull detailed information

about various Super Nintendo games in an effort to repli-
cate aspects of the experience you seek. You can expect
books on various legends (though "Zelda" may be fictional,
The Decameron is thought to be based in reality) and fraternity and brotherhood in contemporary Italian culture
(*Super Mario World*), as well as several CDs of minimalist
synthesizer music with repetitive melodies.

Love,
Dad

The NordicTrack in Your Dad's Office Just Wanted to Say Goodbye

Julie.
What does one say to a lover at the moment when their
mutual exploitation has come to an end? A lover whose flesh
one has used to forget mortality, to pause the march of time,
to deny one's own innate solitude? It would seem that moment
is upon us: the goodbye we both knew was inevitable from
the moment your hungry eyes alit upon my sturdy frame.
For each of our encounters, though we enjoyed delusions of
privacy, was ever more closely observed by a third party, the
reaper of mortal souls that stalked us as if prowling a rocky
Swedish shore in a classic film by a countryman of mine you
are too young to know. Yet my pain at our parting today is
neither unforeseen nor unique. Nay, it is the innate suffering
of man/machine, as inevitable as the eventual slowing of the
heart, in your case, or the decaying of the wood laminate in
mine. It is the lonely ache that lies within all of us conveyed

SUSANNA FOGEL

by the monotonous whoosh of my resistance rotor or your heart's robotic percussion, both tonelessly scoring the mechanical emptiness of life itself.

Forgive me if I sound bleak. As a Scandinavian, I have a predisposition toward fatalism.

And it is undeniable that my entire existence as an exercise machine is one of futility: always moving, but never reaching my destination. Mine is a life confined to basements, windowless "bonus rooms" and, as in your father's case, drawn-curtained home offices whose dim lighting mirrors their occupants' inability to access levity and happiness. I was not merely a bystander to but an active participant in your father's psychological descent. My limbs became additional surface area on which he piled unopened mail, receipts, once even a banana peel. I provided a home for physical manifestations of his mental chaos, while my own existential dread mounted. I collected dust.

Until today, when your father and mother terminated their failed attempt at what was supposed to be an everlasting love of their own and determined that there just wasn't room in your father's new apartment for an exercise machine. When your mother, suddenly panicking about her physical appeal to future partners, decided she would prefer to invest in a new contraption in my stead, the enigmatically named "elliptical," manufactured from soulless synthetics in Stamford, Connecticut. When, after years of broken promises and undiagnosed ailments on your father's part, your mother finally named the isolation she has felt for years. When your father surrendered to an instability for which he secretly loathed himself, a deep pain that only I witnessed whenever he entered his office at dawn under the guise of working on "research," but really to make manic phone calls to old friends who remembered him fondly from childhood, before his circuits began to short. As an object that bore witness to the fracture of your parents' dream of sharing a life, I have come to represent the detritus, the shrapnel of divorce—just as in my youth, two years back in 1993, I represented an exciting new way for everyone to get defined, sexy calves and burn up to nine hundred calories an hour.

Speaking of sexy, then there was you.

You were twelve when we met. I was your plaything, an object of mystification and intrigue. With your baby sister and your wiry-limbed friends, you dabbled, pulled my handles, feigned strangling one another with my ropes (my youth was an era without warning labels, back when lawsuits were for the dignified). But last year, at fourteen, you changed. You grew withdrawn. You talked incessantly of food. You watched television shows that consisted solely of models walking down runways, their eyes seemingly empty sockets. You quit the basketball team. You logged your caloric intake. Friends receded into the deep background. You jogged for hours.

Your parents, despite their differences, discussed in my presence your welfare and whether they should worry. They decided it was fine. They'd keep an eye on it; if it got any worse, they'd take you to a therapist. Only I knew the truth. After midnight, when the house was quiet, I'd wait for the sound of your bare feet at the top of the stairs. I knew it was me you were coming to see. When you climbed astride me, breathtaking in a sports bra and hunter-green knee-length mesh shorts bearing the logo of the Concord Academy Chameleons, our bodies moved together in a perfect rhythm, tiny beads of sweat playing on your upper lip, so stiff with determination. After, I always felt a sense of accomplishment, that this is what I was put on this earth to do. But despite the fact that you returned night after night and spent hours atop me, you took little pleasure in our time together. For you, our love was purely utilitarian, a destructive need driven by hatred for yourself, not love for me. And I, in turn, unwittingly metastasized this cancer. In part, it was our encounters that sent you to the hospital that night in April.

At least we were epic.

Not so epic, I'm afraid, is my disassembly now. I can imagine no more degrading a fate than to be shoved into a Saab hatchback (though at least the make of the car pays tribute to my ancestral home) and later resurrected in the dusty "Electronics/Miscellaneous" section of the Goodwill in Kendall Square, my uniqueness homogenized amidst hot plates and other first-generation electronics whose parts have been discontinued. Yet perhaps this is a poetic end for me. After all, technological progress—like a waning love affair, like the sun disappearing over a Södermalm horizon, like life itself—only moves in one direction.

My power button will now switch to "Off."

—CPS (Classic Pro Skier™)

Your Very Intense Aunt
Just Has a Few House Rules

Dear Julie,

We're all so excited to have you and Jane down to Philadelphia for Thanksgiving next week! I'm so glad we live close enough that we can open our home to you two during this stressful time while your parents are figuring everything out.

In the past, when you've visited here with your family, you've stayed at the DoubleTree, so obviously this trip is going to be a little different. Our family has a few guidelines for guests in our home that help everything run smoothly around here. If you wouldn't mind passing these along to Jane, we would all really appreciate it.

General

Just as a reminder, this is a no-shoes household. Please remove your shoes on the porch and place them on the white rack marked "Guest" before entering the house. Please do not use the mahogany rack—this is for our immediate family. If you are wearing long pants, please check the bottoms to make sure they have not come into contact with any dirt. If they have, just open the front-hall closet and you will find a shelf with a few pairs of clean "house pants" that are for guests to use. You can change in the closet.

Kitchen

I've already been to Natural Foods and bought all the ingredients we need for healthy meals next week. As you

SUSANNA FOGEL

may remember, Paul has two scheduled snacks each day, so between these meals and snacks, there should be no need for you to go into the fridge for any reason during your visit. I would love to avoid a repeat of Memorial Day weekend 1994, when someone in your family left a soy sauce bottle ajar and some soy sauce dripped into the crisper.

Bedrooms

When you make your bed each morning, please tuck the comforter into the bed frame first, then lean all pillows against the headboard in <u>descending order of size</u> (with small circular pillows in the front). Next, please use the French-lavender room spray in the top drawer of the nightstand to freshen up the duvet.

While spraying, please hold the can <u>at least two feet away from the duvet.</u>

Small circular pillows: these should not be slept on, as the fabric is very delicate and contact with any liquid (including any saliva that may escape from your mouth during the night) can cause permanent stains. Please place these pillows in the wicker basket next to the closet before you go to sleep each night.

Bathroom

<u>Please only use the tan towels.</u> The small green towels with Indian-corn embroidery are purely decorative, in honor of the season. If you see any blue towels, do not use them—these towels belong in the master bathroom. There should never be any blue towels in the guest bathroom. If you see

a blue towel in the guest bathroom, please let Carl or me know as soon as possible.

After showering, always make sure to squeegee the shower door to avoid streaking. Please do this **as soon as you turn off the shower** or streaks will set in. **Do not wait until you have toweled off.** If for some reason you forget, please turn the shower back on for 3–5 minutes to re-steam the glass, then squeegee it correctly.

Please do not remove any body hair in the bathroom or anywhere else in the house. This is not typically an issue for our family, as our hair grows fine and blond. If you must remove hair from any part of your body during your visit, please do so in the backyard, using the hose. Since we have been experiencing freezing temperatures this week, please avoid getting any water on the patio, to prevent black ice.

Friday morning

Our family has a tradition of starting the morning after Thanksgiving with a ten-mile run at 7:00 a.m. I know you and Jane aren't athletic types, so we will plan to go without you so no one is slowing anyone down. If you happen to wake up before we get home, feel free to lounge on the living-room couch (please make sure to keep the slipcover on at all times) and watch TV until we get home and can make breakfast as a family. There shouldn't be any need to open the fridge before then. Instructions for the remote controls are in the blue binder under the copy of *Germany: An Ideal Nation.*

Can't wait to see you both Tuesday and give you a few much-needed days of relaxation!

Warmly,
Aunt Andrea (and Carl and Paul)

Your Mother's Goddaughter,
Who Has Always Been Like a Sister to You,
Was a Real Bitch Last Weekend

Dear Julie,

My mom told me you were upset last weekend when you guys came up to visit us and I went to that pool party and didn't invite you. She wanted me to say I'm sorry.

But first of all, I didn't realize you would have wanted to be invited. You always seem like you're morally opposed to anything popular people would want to do. You constantly talk about how you hate makeup and dresses and the only famous person I've ever heard you talking about having a crush on is Bill Clinton, which is obviously weird. Anyway, I'm sure you can understand why I didn't think you would care about having fun with normal high school kids.

I feel comfortable saying this because we've known each other our whole lives and I'm saying it for your own good: in my opinion, if you want to be included in stuff like that, you might want to change some things about how you present yourself to the universe. Here are some ideas I had that I think would majorly improve your life.

<u>If you don't want anything to change in your life, disregard this list.</u>

1. <u>CLOTHES</u>: I know you like to wear used clothes, but some of the outfits you wear just look dirty—like the coat with the fake fur hood that you were wearing last winter when we went down to NY for our moms' college reunion. No offense, but that really just looked like a dog. Maybe that's a popular style at your high school . . . but you don't live very far away from me, so I have a hard time believing it's that different.

2. <u>PERSONALITY</u>: Obviously you have a good sense of humor, but sometimes it gets really annoying that you always have to be joking and making fun of everything. After a while it's not funny anymore. I have definitely talked to a lot of guys who don't like that personality in a girl. Again, maybe it's different at your school, but if it was really that different, you would probably have your own parties to go to on the weekends or would have at least had a boyfriend by now.

3. <u>HOBBIES</u>: Do you have any? Writing doesn't count (I'm only counting hobbies that are social). I recommend sports. In my case, all my friends are on the field hockey team, and it leads to a lot of bonding experiences. Also, when we travel to away games there are parties in other states, which are good opportunities to practice flirting, etc.

4. <u>FRIENDS</u>: I've only ever met one of your friends from school, but my mom said that's the person you hang out with the most. First of all, I can't remember her name, which is a bad sign. All I remember is that she was wheel-

ing her backpack around on a cart with mini Trolls and Koosh balls clipped on to it. Obviously you can understand why someone would think that's queer. So it's also possible that you're not getting invited to things because people don't want to have to invite her. You just have to ask yourself if you'd rather only hang out with her for the next four years or actually expand your social world.

That's it for now. I'll let you know if I think of anything else. Sorry if I hurt your feelings last weekend, but this letter should explain why you can't blame me.

Rachel

PS—If you're not sure how to do any of the above, let me know and next time you guys come up here I could give you a full makeover. I'm sure my friends would help too. Then we could bring the new you to some parties, and I would bet you so much money you would have a totally different experience. Have you seen *Clueless* yet? It's out in the theaters now, and there's a great makeover scene in it we could use for inspiration . . .

Your Eight-Year-Old Sister Had to Write This Letter for School

Dear Julie,

Mrs. Mullen made us write a letter to someone we admire. I admire you because you read a lot of books and you tell funny jokes that make me laugh when I am sad.

How are you? Do you like being in college? Is New York City cold like Boston? Last weekend I slept over Dad's new apartment. He said I could bring a friend and I invited Sage but she had a headache and Dad said no in case its bacterial meningitis. So I went by myself. I got scared in the middle of the night because I heard a loud noise but Dad said it was just drinking college kids. One of them fell asleep on the stairs outside. We had to walk over his legs. Do you like to sleep on the stairs at college?

Dads house isnt as nice as Moms. Dad said thats because Mom steals his money every month even though she has a job too and womens rights shouldnt be a code for men to get screwed in the eyes of Law. I asked Mom why she stole and she got mad because Dad put me in the middle. I dont want to go back to Dads. He spends the whole time in his office and makes me play nintendo in the den. He said im not allowed to go in his office but I went in it yesterday when he was downstairs getting mail. There were a lot of pictures of naked ladies on his computer. One of them looked like our babysitter from Holland but it wasnt her.

Yours Truly,
Jane Feller

Your Hot Cousin Paul and His Friends Might Want to Chill Later

What's up Julie,
Looks like I'm coming down to NYC this weekend with some of my water polo boys—we have interviews on Monday at Merrill Lynch. Not sure about that Wall Street life but any excuse to get the fuck out of Syracuse. Let me know

SUSANNA FOGEL

if there are any chill parties we need to know about on your campus. My mom said you're in a comedy show based on the life of Eleanor Roosevelt on Saturday night—I don't think we'd come to that but let me know if there's an after party.

P

Your Grandma Rose Just Got a Yahoo Account

Hi Julie, It's Grandma Rose and I am writing to let you know my e-mail address is RoseLerner@yahoo.com. They are trying to teach everyone at North Park Village how to use e-mail. They say it will allow us to spend more time with our loved ones.

I don't buy it.

Your Mom, Who Hasn't Seen Your Dad Since the Divorce, Wants to Talk Logistics for Your Graduation Weekend

Hi Jules,
I just wanted to touch base about this weekend.

I still remember dropping you off at your dorm four years ago, watching as my bright, curious girl with wide eyes, ready to take on the world, retreated away from me down a long, hallowed hall filled with history and knowledge that was ready to welcome her with open arms. And now, in just four days, I get to watch a beautiful, intelligent woman stand onstage and revel in all her success and hard work. Honey, I'm kvelling already!

I also wanted to reassure you that I will be completely fine seeing your dad this weekend.

I've worked with so many patients who have very fraught feelings about their ex-spouses. When they interact with them, despite their good intentions, they are unable to control themselves and put aside their own "baggage" and resentments. I would never want to put you in that position at such an important and memorable time in your life.

That's why I have been working on a "schedule" to ensure that your dad and I won't have to interact at any point other than at the ceremony itself. That way, neither he nor I will run the risk that the tension and unresolved angst that remains (and always will) between us will threaten the happy memories you deserve to make!

I hope this makes you feel less nervous about the weekend.

Love,

Mom

Your Dad, Who Hasn't Seen Your Mom Since the Divorce, Wants to Talk Logistics for Your Graduation Weekend

Dear Julie,
It was with great pride that I received an e-mail from your university that you have made their dean's list.

Ordinarily, I would say this foretells an advantage for

you in the job market, but given that you have chosen to pursue a career in creative writing, the accomplishment is probably irrelevant from a practical standpoint.

Still, a nice feather in your cap.

I also received my invitation to your commencement ceremony. I eagerly await a weekend of celebration, reflection, and reconnecting with your mother now that several years have passed since our divorce. I assume any resentment on her end is water under the bridge and that she has been enjoying as active a dating life as I have. I look forward to exchanging anecdotes with her, along with a laugh over how woefully mismatched we were as a couple.

The naïveté of youth!

Love,
Dad

Your Fourteen-Year-Old Sister, Who Is Dating a Seventeen Year Old, Can't Wait for Her First Trip to New York

Dear Julie!
Hi! I can't wait to see you this weekend at yr graduation! How excited are you? And mom said you made a Deans List? I have no idea what that is but it sounds cool!!!!!!

How weird is it gonna be to see Mom and Dad together again?!?!?!?!?!?!!?

Mom keeps telling me she's fine with it but every night she has been staying up all night watching some tv show about unsolved murders???????? I'm like are you taking notes so you can kill Dad???!!! hahahaha. Don't worry I will sit in between them during your graduation just in case . . . (I have been taking karate . . .)

I also have a small favor to ask—I know u will be busy graduating but is there any way you would also have some time to take me to get a fake ID in Times Square this weekend? (NOT FOR DRINKING!!!! Just so I can go to this club on Lansdowne St. that is 18+! But Ammar said I should get it for age 21 anyway just to keep our options open.) Maybe we could tell Mom we are going to a museum or something? Haha except its me so she would know that's a lie! But we could come up with something else. Let me know!!!!!

xoxoxoxo

Jane

Ps—I think I might have sex with Ammar soon wish me luck!

Your Favorite '90s Musicians Would Like to Drop Some Knowledge on You

Hey friend,
Amy Ray and Emily Saliers here—we don't have to tell you we're also known as the Indigo Girls. This is your favorite album. That's why you're listening to it today, on your graduation day, while you pack up your dorm room to start your new life. We're super honored to provide the soundtrack

for your—okay, we were about to say "rite of passage," but it felt a little obvious. As you know, we prefer metaphors that really make you think.

We've gotta keep this short. We're trying to reach out to all the girls who are listening to us on their graduation days. Maybe that's a little ambitious since that's more than three million letters, but we figure if anyone has enough power to make it happen, it's us.

We'd say we're like Santa Claus, except as you can imagine we're not super into organized religion.

So we'll get to it: Your parents just left. You wish they hadn't, even though you told them to. You just needed to be alone. Or that's what you thought you wanted. Now you feel too alone. But they shouldn't have had that fight at the restaurant last night. That dinner was supposed to be a celebration—this whole weekend was. Hey, Julie, you know what? That just wasn't about you. That's *their* stuff, their history. You can't take on the burdens, the resentments, the mistakes of those who came before you. Seriously, we have so many songs about this.

Still, you could have used their advice. Your real life is about to start, and it seems like it might be terrible. Your new apartment, above a cigar shop in Long Island City, doesn't even have a working shower. Your new roommate is someone from your psych class that you don't even like that much. You don't have a job yet, and Big Apple Staffing said things are always slow in the summer. What if they never call, and you have no choice but to move back home to Boston? What if you're too depressed to write anything ever again? What if nothing about you ends up being special, and then you die an unremarkable death?

Girl, we get it. Life is scary stuff. But the good news is there's no one right way to live it. There's more than one answer to these questions pointing you in a crooked line. Not trying to be narcissistic there, we just can't think of any better or more resonant way to phrase it. I mean, can you?

Gotta run now, Julie. We're heading up to Sarah Lawrence after this, and that stop's going to take hours. But hang in there, okay? We love you.

Amy and Emily

Your Fifteen-Year-Old Sister Has Some Tips on How to Blow Your Guy's Mind

Hi Julie!!!!!!!!!!!!!!!
Thank you for sending me the most beautiful purse in the world for my birthday I love it and I am using it every day! (even though I have like no money to put in it haha). You are the best sister on planet earth! And it really means a lot cuz I know u don't make a lot of money in yr receptionist job.

Ammar is sitting next to me right now and he wants me to thank u from him too because the purse reminds him of something Carmen Electra would use and she is his celebrity crush!!!!

How is being out of college? Im so jealous u are done with school forever LOL. Even tho I know yr job sucks and u don't have enough time to write. U will figure it out.

How are things going with Matt? I know u said u guys were having problems because he felt too much pressure being your first boyfriend—but Ammar said that sounds like bullshit. He said normal guys love being the first so he thinks Matt is probably gay. But I think maybe he just feels like yr not experienced enough in bed so he is starting to look around but really doesn't want to hurt u?

Anyway just in case you are curious about some tips on how to rock his world—CALL ME!!!!! I have one that Ammar and I discovered that always gets results LOL. It involves a grapefruit . . .

Ugh gotta go mom is kicking Ammar out cuz she wants me to do my homework that woman is crazy more later I LOVE YOU SISTERRRRRRRR!!!

—J-Slice

Your Mom
Does Not Need You to Write Her Back!

Hi sweetie,

I'm sending this regular mail because I'm staying off my e-mail for now. Some weird things have been happening with my account. I got a very strange message last week from an anonymous address—I won't tell you what it said because I don't want to embarrass you, but let's just say it was clearly intended to be provocative. I called the Apple Store and made an appointment for tomorrow so they can take a look at my computer and reprogram it so I don't get any more of these. The writer actually seems like he or she might be mentally disturbed. There were all sorts of big letters and different colors and then the whole thing is apparently trying to get me to buy something you clip on to the side of your penis? Or, you know, not *your* penis. A man's penis. I really don't know how they got ahold of my e-mail address.

Before I go on, I just wanted to say don't feel any pressure to reply. I've been thinking about the conversation we had last time I visited you, when you took me to that little bar you and your friends like and you said it seems like I need us to be best friends and it makes you feel like a bad daughter. Honey, I don't know where you got the impression that I have those kinds of expectations. I have a very full life here in Newton. I've been spending a lot of time at Temple Emanuel, and they have so many concerts and activities I'm getting involved in. Of course, most of the women my age there are married, but it's not like they pity me or anything—except occasionally around the holidays. Anyway, want to hear something fun? My friend Ruth's husband David wants to fix me up with a man from his work! The only thing is David thinks he might have cancer. We're going to figure out what kind of cancer it is. I'll keep you posted.

Other than that, I've been having a blast working on my little roof garden! Or trying: it's about ten degrees out. Last week there was some black ice on the deck and I had a fall, but don't worry! I'm fine now. They only made me stay at the hospital one night. I thought about calling you, but I know how busy you are, so I just figured if you happened

SUSANNA FOGEL

to call me to say hi I'd tell you. It's funny—the whole time I was lying on that cot at Mass General, I kept thinking, this never would have happened if I lived near Julie! But obviously that's just a hypothetical. I was only thinking about that because I'm getting into gardening. I really do have a lot going on here. I just signed up to volunteer for the Democratic Party, so that's been a lot of fun.

That reminds me: the Democratic Party gave us a sign-up sheet for volunteering. I told them I had to check your schedule—I don't want them depending on me if you want me to come visit. Don't worry: I'll book a hotel room this time! I remember at the bar that night, you said you felt weird sleeping in the same bed with your mother now that you're in your late twenties. I'm so glad we have the kind of relationship where you can be honest with me. I'll get a room at the Westin. And I'll make sure it has two beds in case you want to sleep there too. Of course, if you'd rather go home at the end of the night I'd understand, but if you wanted to have a glass of wine and not have to worry about getting all the way back to Queens, we could have a little slumber party at the hotel and then the next morning we could get up and go for a walk in Central Park and then a light lunch and maybe to a museum and/or shopping and then a nice cozy dinner somewhere. But only if that works for you.

One last thing. I'm sending you a little package from Mail Boxes Etcetera. It's a box of cards I bought at Brook-line Booksmith; they're blank inside but on the outside are these beautiful paintings. They're very European, almost medieval. There's a quote on the front: "A friend is a second self."—Cicero. They remind me of that summer we traveled to Florence before your first year of high school, right before we found out about Dad and the IRS. That may have been the best two weeks of my life. But don't feel obligated to send me a card! Of course, if you did, I'd put it on the fridge; you just shouldn't feel any pressure because I already have a lot of cards on my fridge. I just added a really nice one from Dianne Feinstein. Well, not Dianne Feinstein herself; it's from her office. I donated to her campaign, even though I don't live in California. I'm just very impressed (and proud!) of all she's been able to accomplish as a Jewish woman. The card has a picture of her whole family sitting by the fireplace. They seem really close-knit. I heard an interview with her on All Things Considered and she was saying she and her daughter talk every day.

Okay, honey, it's getting late here. Time to brush my teeth and watch an episode of *Law & Order: SVU* and hit the sack. There was an interesting episode on last night about parents who hadn't heard from their daughter in a week. They thought she was just busy at work, but it turned out a sociopathic man had kidnapped her and tied her up in a basement and only untied her when he was forcing her to mutilate herself and some small children. It was very suspenseful. I think you'd appreciate the writing. I'll try to record it on my DVR so that next time you visit here we can watch it together.

With so much love,
Mom

SUSANNA FOGEL

Your Sister Said Something Racist to Your Dad's New Girlfriend

Hey Jules,

Just tried u but got yr voice mail. So I just met the lady dad is dating . . . did u know she is Chinese? Not that I care, I mean my new boyfriend Carlos is puerto rican and I think his grandma is part Cherokee, I'm just sayin I think its kinda weird Dad never mentioned that???? anyway ugh this part is so embarrassing . . . so I was supposed to go over to his place to meet her and have dinner and I walk in and they had ordered all this chinese food and I go IT SMELLS LIKE CHINESE and then this fucking chinese woman walks into the room! she's all Hi I'm May Ling nice to meet you! And like I didn't say Chinese FOOD when I walked in—I just said it smells like Chinese . . . so then the whole night I was like oh fuck does she think I'm a racist now?!?!?!? Thanks for the warning dad.

Another fucked up thing dad did . . . last weekend we were having one of our awkward lunches we are forced to have every other week since the divorce haha and I tell him I need some $$$$ to get a new raincoat bc I am supposed to go camping with carlos soon. then dad suddenly gets super obsessed with driving me to the REI outlet. I was confused cause u know Dad and there is no way he needs anything at an athletic store. But then he gets off at this random exit and drives onto a random college campus!! I think its called Tufts. He's all AS LONG AS WE'RE DRIVING BY WE MIGHT AS WELL TAKE A TOUR!!!! Ugh real subtle dude. then these super jewish dudes with yamakas (sp?)

walk by talking about like physics and I'm like dad are you blind these are so not my people! just bc of the science shit not bc of the yamakas haha. Ok how many racist things can I say in one email???? Lololol but seriously. My grades and test scores suck and I am counting down the days till I graduate HS next year. its like dude sorry but you may end up only having one daughter who grows up to be a nerd. haha no offense.

Meanwhile moms all HONEY I WILL BE PROUD OF YOU NO MATTER WHAT PATH YOU CHOOSE. Like I could become a drug dealer and she would be sending out newsletters to her friends bragging like you guys my beautiful daughter sold 8 kilos of cocaine this month! Haha. So weird they ever got married!!!!

Call meeeeeeeeee

Jane

Your Grandma Rose Just Heard about Your Dad's New Fiancée

Julie, I hear your father is engaged to someone new already. What's the matter with him? I guess I'm not surprised. Well, if you want to know what I'm really surprised about, I'm surprised it's a woman. I always had a funny feeling about your dad.

Your Dad, a 50-Something Neurologist, Can't Fucking Wait for His Bachelor Party

Dear Julie,

It appears that I will be in your neck of the woods on April 18.

As you may recall, Martin Rothman, my best friend from Yale, is now a Manhattan-based historian who studies the evolution of Soviet forced-labor camps. He was thrilled to hear about my upcoming nuptials and generously offered to host a gendered gathering in my honor, though I will refrain from using the phrase "bachelor party" since, as I'm sure you can guess, I am wary of any event that celebrates a descent into Bacchanalian behavior.

That said, I am theoretically amenable to the idea of "having fun."

I will be meeting several male acquaintances in front of the Lichtenstein in the south wing of the Museum of Modern Art at noon. I felt this was a fitting meeting place, as Roy Lichtenstein's work also serves as a potent metaphor for the randomness and ineffability of true love. We will then enjoy a cocktail or two at the Yale Club. Finally, as is customary at these events, we will attend a performance by the American Ballet Theatre—dancing that is, indeed, "exotic" in its discipline and rigor.

If your schedule allows and you would like to meet me for dinner afterward, plans are in the works to connect with Mei-Ling and her cousin Wen, an aspiring comedienne from Beijing who's in the States studying sketch comedy at the Upright Citizens Brigade Theatre. Let me know. The venue is a restaurant in Chinatown by the name of 明代故宫 that comes highly regarded by the natives. There is no English translation or sign, but all the many restaurants in that area have Mandarin characters printed on the building's façade, so you shouldn't have any trouble distinguishing this one.

Also, I will not be extending this invitation to your sister, as I'm reluctant to distract Jane in any way from her schoolwork. That said, I'm pleased to report that I think she really enjoyed our recent visit to Tufts and agreed with me that it could be a perfect fit for her.

How goes your progress with the Great American Novel?

Love,
Dad

Your Mom, Who Just Found Out
Your Dad Is Getting Remarried,
Is Really Ready to Get Back Out There

Hi sweetie,
Thank you for your e-mail letting me know your dad has decided to get remarried. I just want you to know that I'm fine. I've always been a very resilient person. I'm a little surprised, given how often he used to talk about how he thought the institution of marriage was outdated, but it's none of my business.

This must be something his fiancée is insisting on due to her cultural background and the expectations and norms for Chinese women. According to the stories Dr. Leung tells me when I go in to get my dental work done, it can be a very rigid culture when it comes to expectations for women, especially women of a certain age. I'm just so happy that at this point in my life I don't feel obligated to do or be anything I don't want to do or be. I can feel free to make wonderful connections with people without the pressure to conform.

I've never been a conformist.

In fact, I have the pictures to prove it! Just the other day, I was looking through an album of old photos from my college theater troupe, which was founded in 1968 to create plays to protest the Vietnam War. We called ourselves the Characters of Conflict.

I've attached one of the photos if you're curious to see me in action. In this picture, I'm in the middle of my monologue as Lady Macbeth—even though, as you can see, I'm wearing a Richard Nixon mask.

Also, if you "zoom in" on the back left corner of the photo, the man staring at his own reflection in the mirror is Art Garfunkel. Wherever we performed, Art would always find a mirror. You can probably guess what his personality was like.

Still, he was a very good kisser!

I hope it doesn't make you uncomfortable that I just shared that with you. Art Garfunkel never became my boyfriend, but as you can imagine, at that moment in history emotions and passions were running high.

Looking at this picture of Art Garfunkel, I can't help but remember how it felt to just experiment and explore and find new ways to express ourselves. I feel inspired to reach out to men who have a similar background to mine, with similar ideals, to see if I could make a connection with one of them. My friend Rena, from temple (I left you a message last week about a wonderful exhibit of sculpture we saw together about the Diaspora), told me about a retreat in Tanglewood for single people my age who were once activists or involved in political movements. I think I may sign up. I'll keep you posted. Wouldn't it be wild if I ran into one of the other Characters?

I'll let you know how it goes.

Give me a call this weekend if you have some time. I would love to hear how everything is going at work. Were you able to get the office manager to stop making those comments about your body? Feel free to tell him your mother's from the Bronx and she's not afraid to give anyone a knuckle sandwich!

Love,
Mom

Your Mom
Found the Singles Retreat She Just Attended Problematic

Hi sweetheart,
I tried to leave you a voice mail but the woman in your phone told me your mailbox was full. Give me a call when you get a chance. I'd love to tell you about my weekend at Tanglewood at the Activist Singles Retreat.

It was not what I thought it would be.

Maybe it's because I've been disconnected from the activist community since I was an undergraduate (except for my yearly contributions to Dianne Feinstein, who I've always thought of as a real "kindred spirit"), but I found the people at this retreat to be quite angry and discontented with their lives.

I also felt like I was "on the clock"—as a therapist, I couldn't help but find myself listening to most of the men I met and talking them through ways to manage and process their anger. I felt reserved about admitting any of my own vulnerabilities. I was hoping I'd have a chance to let it all hang out during the sing-along, but it turned out the songs we sang were mostly about oppression and set a bit of a somber tone (though slave spirituals are often beautiful and inspiring in their own right, in terms of what they represent and the melodies themselves).

On the bright side, I did get a chance to see how many of these men handle conflict under pressure. At dinner, an argument broke out between those who opted for the barbecued meat that was served and those who were staunch vegetarians and believed it was hypocritical for any activist to be otherwise. The debate became quite heated, and many of the men who had otherwise seemed quite relaxed became enraged, showing a side of themselves I wouldn't want to touch with a ten-foot pole, much less feel comfortable being intimate around!

One man in particular, who I had had my eye on, turned out to have a very unintegrated idea about how to channel his anger. His name was Lewis. Earlier in the day, during the group hike, I had found myself drawn to him because he had a very kind face. Unfortunately, during the conflict at dinner, he began hurling epithets at the organizer of the retreat that showed a very ugly side of him. Something clicked in me and I stopped seeing his face as attractive at all.

This could also be partly due to the fact that, as I later learned, most of Lewis's features were reconstructed. His face was very badly burned in 1972 after he blew up a science lab that was testing nuclear weapons. I found it telling that, as a Jewish man, he had chosen conventionally "WASPy" features to replace his previous features, which suggests some deeper issues of self-loathing about a heritage I am very proud of! No thanks!

But I don't want you to worry that this was a traumatic experience for me. I actually appreciated how effective the activist retreat was as a sort of "speed dating," expediting the process of seeing how potential partners would deal with opposition and how receptive they would be to other views. Unfortunately, in this case it seemed that most people at this retreat were unable to accept any opinions that were different from their own—which sounds a lot like someone we both know who I was already married to for twenty years!

So I guess it's back to the drawing board, but at least now I feel ready to draw.

With so much love,
Mom

Your Dad Has Some Feedback on the Wedding Toast You Gave

Julie and Jane,

Thank you for making the trip to Cambridge to attend my nuptials last week. It was, without contest, the happiest day of my life, and I was thrilled to be able to share it with my daughters, biological and otherwise.

Specifically, Jane, I wanted to praise your command of rhythm and meter as you recited the Milton quotation I picked out for you. It gave your speech a very personal touch, though in fairness, that person was John Milton.

And, Julie, your comedic timing was equally impressive in your impromptu "roast" of me—though I'll admit I don't remember the anecdote you recalled from your youth, in which you threw your stuffed animals down the stairs while bellowing "Animal brigade!" and I, in turn, allegedly imitated the sounds of the various species of animal as they appeared at my feet. Although a charming story, it may have disturbed some of Mei-Ling's guests, as upper-class Chinese families generally do not encourage this kind of chaos in their child-rearing. That said, your delivery evoked a young Gilda Radner, as did your manelike shock of hair that stood out amidst the sea of smooth, shiny locks native to those of Asian descent.

Now, ready those refrigerator magnets—postcards from our honeymoon to the ancient shrines of Japan are forthcoming.

Love,
Dad

Your Sister Thinks Your Dad's Speech Was Bullshit

Jules u online?
I just read Dad's email and got super fuckin pissed all over
again. "Biological and otherwise"? Thanks for reminding
me of that wonderful memory of you telling a room full of
randomass people from China that I was adopted!!! It's just
rude. Not that most of the people there even understood his
speech lol.

At least now I don't feel as bad telling him I'm not going
to college. I'm gonna call him now and tell him I have
chosen to do OTHERWISE with my life!!!!!

OK u are not there . . . if i dont text you later tonight just
assume he murdered me . . .

xo

Your Dad's Friend Who Makes You a Little Uncomfortable Thought It Was Great Seeing You

Dear Julie,
Thank you for approving my friend request. It was such a
pleasure talking to you at your dad's wedding. And a relief!
You never know who you're going to get stuck sitting next
to at these things. I'm sure you felt the same way when you
found out you were seated next to me—even though, as I
said when you sat down, I didn't recognize you at first since
I hadn't seen you since you were a little girl. I know I'm a

SUSANNA FOGEL

doctor, so the miracles of the human body shouldn't surprise me, but what a difference a few years makes.

Anyway, I really enjoyed hearing a little bit about your life in New York and your budding writing career and I wanted to extend an invitation to you: I'd like to offer up my guesthouse on Nantucket any time you want to get out of the city for a little writer's retreat. As you may remember from visiting me in the summer with your family when your parents were still married (as was I, to a woman who never really understood me), the guesthouse is just a few yards from the main house, where I now live year-round. Among other amenities, it has a full bathroom with a Jacuzzi tub and a trail right out the back door to a private pond. My daughter and her friends always find it very comfortable when they come down from Bard for the weekend. I think I mentioned she's abroad in Madrid this semester. Speaking of Alicia, she always leaves a few outfits in the guest-room dresser, so if you decide to come at the last minute and don't have time to pack, I'm sure she wouldn't mind you wearing them. She's about your size, though I think your waist is a little smaller.

Suffice it to say, the compound is a great place to find inspiration—very Henry David Thoreau. Though I'm not a writer, I once wrote an ode to the island that was featured in the *Dartmouth Alumni Magazine*. Speaking of Dartmouth, it also occurred to me that I have several friends from college who are professional writers and might be able to advise you or help you get a writing job. I know how hard it is to make those initial contacts. If you do end up taking me up on my offer, maybe we could take a walk in the woods one afternoon and chat about what introductions you'd like me to make. I should also mention that if travel costs are an issue, I'd be happy to help you out with airfare. I know how important it is to have a Room of One's Own, so to speak, while trying to be creative. I've always been a big fan of Virginia Woolf myself. What can I say? I'm a feminist.

Which reminds me: I also keep an extensive collection of records from some of the grand dames of jazz in the main house. If you come during the winter, when it's snowing, there's really nothing like making a fire in the fireplace, cracking open a bottle of Malbec (I still have a case in the shed from a medical conference I attended in Argentina—I was the keynote speaker for my work on precancerous moles), putting on an old Lena Horne LP, and just letting yourself get lost. Not that I only like old music. I enjoy a lot of new stuff too—I have several new-music stations programmed into my satellite radio. I once introduced my daughter to a track by Belle and Sebastian she'd never even heard of. As you may have gathered by now, I'm not exactly your typical dad. In fact, I can't remember the last time anyone called me that. Everyone just calls me Larry, even Alicia.

Anyway, I should sign off now. Diane Sawyer (whose house is down the road—if you take me up on my offer, I'm happy to make an introduction) flew in a sushi chef from New York to teach a few of us locals how to make rolls. I always say yes to new experiences. Something tells me you're a kindred spirit . . .

Fondly,
Larry (Shepherd)

PS—If memory serves, you always loved horses. My friend down the road owns two Arabians. If you wanted to go riding, I could make that happen.

SUSANNA FOGEL

Your Asian Stepmother
Would Like to Reassure You
That Your Dad Doesn't Have a Power Thing

To My Stepdaughter Julie,

This is Mei-Ling. Your father and myself appreciated you at our wedding very much and just received your special red pot from the list to which we registered at Macy's. It is very beautiful and practical—when you make your next visit home, I will cook dinner for all of us in the pot. I am looking forward to truly getting to know you better, as I know it was not fortunate that we had such a little time to spend before the wedding occurred. The sunny side is that we are now in a family and can all find love and intimacy together.

There also exists another topic that I wish to confess, more personal in nature. Since living in America, I have been observant of the American's thinking that white men loving women from Asia must have strange sexual tendencies or power ideas. It is a possibility that other men find this true. However, I do not want you to worry about your father. He has no fetish. We make love that is quite simple and similar from time to time. Only mission style, and sometime he fall asleep in center of sex. Efforts are made often and his energy is ambitious, but the end product far from blows minds. So, I hope you aren't concerning yourself with this.

Once again, I look forward very much to gathering with you for a pot dinner soon.

Yours truly,
Mei-Ling Feller

The Gerbil You Drowned in 1990
Would Like a Word with You

Hi, you fucking bitch.

Oh, I'm sorry, was that a harsh opener? Do I give a shit? Bet you forgot all about me, didn't you? Well, here I am, after fifteen years, to remind you. Did you know gerbils have memories like elephants? Guess what? They don't. Know who does, though? Dead gerbils in fucking heaven with nothing to do all day but replay every second of our short, miserable lives, some made even more miserable by little eight-year-old shits who aren't ready for the responsibility of the puppy they asked for. Was that why you did it? Because I was just some goddamned consolation prize? I hope you never got that dog. Then I hope you try to have kids later in life, and it turns out you're infertile. That's what someone like you deserves.

I'm not a gerbil who believes in regret. If I did, I'd say I fucked up the second I decided to trust you. I don't know, you just honestly didn't seem like a fucking murderer to me. When you walked into the Pet Depot on that spring day in '90 in those little terrycloth shorts and your Rainbow Brite shirt, the faint remains of chicken pox on your angelic little fucking face, every single one of us in that cage wanted to go home and snuggle the shit out of you while you learned long division. I was just the only motherfucker smart enough to do a backflip when I knew your mom was looking 'cause I knew she'd eat that shit up. And when it was me you carried out of the store to your Dodge Caravan, I didn't look back through that little glass box once at my

SUSANNA FOGEL

brethren. I was like, sayonara, bitches! Guess I laughed all the way to my untimely fucking death, didn't I?

Who gave you the idea for a "Gerbil Olympics," anyway? What kind of Olympics has one fucking contestant? And who even cares about the fucking swimming competition in the Olympics? You drop a motherfucker in ten inches of water for what—just to show off for some little ginger kid with a lisp? What was his name again? Lo and behold, I don't give a shit. All I know is that the last thing I heard as I choked on mouthfuls of tepid bathwater laced with the bitter residue of No More Tears baby shampoo was him screaming at the top of his tiny little lungs. I hope he never spoke to you again, then became a fucking male model. What are you planning on doing with your life now, by the way? Border Patrol have any openings? Slaughterhouse technician? Nazi work camp reenactments? No, really, I'm dying to know.

Sorry, did you want to defend yourself? You were just a kid? It was an accident? There are worse ways to die? Not that it's any of your fucking business, but yeah, sure, what happened to some of my friends up here was just as bad. My boy Pepper went blind after some fucking scientist at Maybelline or some shit poured mascara in his eyes. And some stoned idiot fed my ex, Darth Vader (yeah, that's right, he was too high to realize she was a fucking girl), to his fucking boa constrictor. You know why? Because no one cares about us, ever. It's like my buddy Morgan—this wise, old dark-brown gerbil up here—always says: a gerbil's life is a life of assholes. Either assholes are putting stuff in us or we're getting put in assholes—literally. Just in case you ever felt like walking a mile in anyone's shoes but your own, which I highly fucking doubt.

At least I can fall asleep at night knowing you still have to walk around the planet as a sociopath, while I get to chill up here all day sipping on nail polish remover. Because guess what? That shit may be toxic, but it actually tastes pretty fucking delicious. Guess what else? Even though I died a virgin thanks to you, I get the last laugh there too. The second I got here, there were seventy-two virgin gerbils at my disposal, because our entire lives are god-damned suicide missions. Now we get to fuck like rabbits all day. Sometimes, if you're a baller like me, we fuck actual rabbits.

Glug, glug, glug. Remind you of anyone you killed, dying? May that sound haunt your dreams tonight, psycho.

Rocket Feller (1989–1990)

Your Sister in Arizona, Who Owns Guns, Doesn't Understand Your Taste in Men

heya not sure if you even use FB chat but i just noticed you changed your relationship status to single ☹ sorry gurrrrl but can i say i always thought that dude was hella weird? i know you always say guys in nyc are different than here in arizona and I don't get it but he always just seemed like a pussy to me haha. sorry but its just straight up weird that he went to coffee tastings (???) and all he talked about was weird bands no one's ever heard of. and remember when i was visiting you and he kept giving me shit just cause i buy stuff from informercials (sp?). like who even cares dude you wear womens jeans. you just deserve hella better. i know you love the nyc life but if you ever moved to scottsdale you would get treated like a queen. just come down for a weekend at least and you can meet my hot neighbor mike whos a fireman and he just got divorced (he posts on my FB a lot if you wanna see pix). he thinks your cute too. check out the pic where hes straight up saving a cat out of a tree. YOU COULD BE THAT PUSSY hehe. sorry now im just being gross i love you hunny hang in there

xoxoxoxoox

Your Dad Would Like to Chime In about Your Latest Breakup

Dear Julie,

I spoke to your sister this afternoon to wish her a happy birthday. She mentioned that you and Miles decided to part ways.

I'm not surprised. I never felt Miles was right for you and always predicted this would happen.

Perhaps I made a mistake in not telling you at the time what was so obvious to everyone else. Next time, I will make sure to let you know my honest thoughts on your boyfriends as soon as I meet them, so you don't waste as much time.

Love,
Dad

Your Grandma Rose Is Still
Not Feeling This E-mail Thing

Julie, I still don't get this. This is supposed to be time with you? I'm sitting here staring at a robot. Is this just the way of the world now? Some people here don't mind. Maureen, who lives down the hall, has practically moved into the computer lab. She spends all day talking to her family on a video. Every night at dinner, she tells us about their lives as if any of us knows any of the people she's talking about. Maureen's a real dodo. She wears high heels every day even though none of us really leaves the building. Who is she trying to impress? God? That's the other thing about Maureen—she's very Catholic. Enough said.

Your Uncle Ken, Who Has Never Had a Girlfriend, Is Loving His Trip to Disney World

Heya, Family Feller!
Greetings from sunny Florida! I hope you're all having a great holiday break. I know I am, just sitting here soaking up the tropical air and drinking Arnold Palmers by the pool. I feel like I'm on Gilligan's Island! Or make that Treasure Island—the pool here at the hotel is built like a giant lagoon in the shape of mouse ears. Pretty neat.

I attached a file courtesy of Walt Disney & Co. Don't worry—it's not SPAM! It's just a little advent calendar featuring Mickey and the rest of the gang. I know we're Jewish, but I just thought it was fun, and they didn't have a

Hanukkah version. They did put up a big menorah by Splash Mountain this year, so that's something!

Sending hugs,
Uncle Ken

PS—I just found out one of my students is a state quarterfinalist for the Rocky Mountain Science Prize! All my kids are really kicking butt this year.

Your Sister,
Who Has Questions about Your Uncle's Lifestyle,
Has a Great Idea for His Birthday Gift

HEY GIRL HEY.

OK . . . i am gunna cut to the chase. u know how we think uncle Ken might be a virgin?

i know we have not discussed this for a couple yrs but I srsly doubt things have changed for that dude since then. like hes still saying innocent shit all the time like OH GOSH and JEEZ LOUISE haha. for real i know he's a high school teacher so he is probably not allowed to swear at work but still what grown man says gosh who is not like a professional clown??? and remember last thanksgiving when we were watchin jeopardy after dinner and you asked if ppl wanted to watch something on hbo and he said he doesn't even get hbo cause he doesn't like watching "all that sexy stuff"!?!!!! like wtf are you afraid of seeing?! there is only one answer to that question . . . POON.

also lets be real here there is no way he has a woman in

his life or she wd have pointed out that his pants are always like six inches too short and ugh his turtlenecks with all his dandruff on the shoulders. u would at least think his roommate wd point it out . . .

that's the other thing—who has a fuckin roommate at his age?!

i am saying this out of concern for the man, u know i think Ken is srsly the sweetest person. remember when i went to stay with him by myself when mom n dad were workin their shit out (unsuccessfully, ha) and he taught me that song so i could remember all the planets in the solar system? the one time I actually got an A on a test LOL.

ok I promise there is a point to this email. so i was in vegas last wknd with kyle (guy I texted you about that I met last month @ gas station)? It was kind of a fuckin nightmare cause i thought we were gunna do fun stuff but all he wanted to do is spend the whole time at this weird illegal dogfight (??? Don't ask—why do i pick these men??????) and as u know i am really into animal rights so i couldn't fuckin deal . . . so i ended up just hangin at our hotel bar getting trashed solo. it actually turned out to be a blessing in disguise cuz I met this really nice girl at the bar. her name is Bree and we started chatting and ended up chillin the whole night and going to PF Changs together cause she knows the manager and he gave us tons of free shit. Anyway soooooooo it actually turned out Bree is a hooker????? and she was in the middle of telling me that she just had sex with this older dude who was a virgin and it sparked an idea since Ken's 50th bday is coming up . . . u can probly see where i am going with this . . .

SUSANNA FOGEL

SHOULD WE HIRE BREE FOR UNCLE KENS BDAY ANONYMOUSLY??!?!?!

if he really is a virgin this wd solve his entire life. and it wd never get traced back to us. Ken would never suspect us. if anything he wd probably just think one of the other teachers at his school did it or his roommate or whatever, or one of the guys he plays in that indoor racket ball (sp?) league with. (btw racket ball=more evidence). all we wd have to do is pay for Bree to drive to denver and show up @ his house. I already asked her what the price wd be and she said she would do it for $250 and we laughed about how it is another meaning of the saying FRIENDS AND FAMILY RATE. srsly i really think Ken wd be into her. you know how he has that pic of that black and white actress on his fridge? i forget her name but Bree kinda looks like her a little bit. and shes not like super young shes middle aged . . . i think shes like 33?

OMG AND GUESS WHAT ELSE I CANT BELIEVE I FORGOT TO MENTION THISSSSSSS she loves jeopardy and she actually remembers when uncle Ken was on it!!!!!!!

OMGOMGOMG what if they fall in love and then next thxgiving uncle Ken brings her home to moms and hes like everyone meet my girlfriend she's a brain surgeon or whatever and only we know the secret . . . !!!

kk ill stop till I hear back from you but if u wanna check Bree out i attached a link to her FB here. fuck is that illegal since i am not in Nevada right now where sex slavery is allowed or whatever? I am so not trying to get arrested right now. Whatev, ill be like officer i plead guilty of trying to make sure my favorite uncle doesn't die a fuckin virgin! then I wd just have uncle Ken come down to the station to testify and the cop would take one look at him and be like oh ok I get it jane u are free to go hahaha.

no but for real dude think about this proposal cuz i seriously think im a genius.

love

me

Ps—what if the joke is actually on us and uncle Ken is one of those super dorky dudes who secretly goes to sex dungeons and does super fucked up shit in his spare time like hanging from the ceiling from his nipples hahahaha omg why did I just give myself that mental image . . .

Your Mother's Goddaughter,
Who Crashed with You for Many Days,
Is Sorry She Didn't Have Any Time to Hang Out

J,

I think you're still asleep so just leaving you this note. Thanks for letting Ellie and I crash @ your apartment! We had a great time in NYC. Best long weekend ever.

Sucks we didn't get to hang out at all! I just had a lot of people to see in the city, including a bunch of friends from my year abroad in London who live here now. They have really tight schedules because they're all doing really cool things here.

Sorry about the confusion last night btw—I thought we had said we MIGHT meet you at that pub after dinner, but I guess you thought that was a set plan. Anyway, hope you weren't waiting too long. We ended up at this crazy house party in the W. Village that turned out to be Mischa Barton from *The O.C.*'s apartment. Not sure if you watch that show but she's like ridiculously beautiful. Anyway, we were there till like 4:00 a.m. and by the time I got home and got your voice mails (my phone was dead) you were asleep!

See ya soon—maybe when we're both home for Passover (my mom said your mom wants to host a seder together?) if I end up going. I might be going to St. Lucia with my friend Cait.

R

PS—I think we used all the toilet paper in your loo (aka bathroom—I still use all these English words and phrases from my year abroad).

Your Grandma Rose Isn't So Sure about California

Julie, I heard you're leaving New York and moving to LA. Why are you doing that? You're a smart girl.

Don't tell me there's a man in the picture. There are plenty of men around here, and they have a lot more going on upstairs, if you know what I mean.

Your Dad, Who Was a Doctor by Twenty-Five, Just Heard about Your Entry-Level Day Job

Julie,

I just visited Dr. Leung, who as you know also continues to have your mother as a dental patient. She alerted me that you have acquired a position as a contributor at the *Huffington Post* and will be relocating to Los Angeles accordingly. While I have always found Arianna Huffington's view of international politics reductive and her pan-European accent cacophonous, I have no doubt that your "beat" writing quotidian updates about celebrities will require minimal mental exertion, preserving your energies for more creative pursuits. Mazel tov.

Dad

Your Mom Thinks You Should Be Very Proud!

Hi sweetheart!

How are you settling in to life in LA? I just tried to send you a text message from my computer using "I Messages" like you showed me, but I'm in Denver visiting Uncle Ken and I don't think that program works in Colorado. I'm going to see if Ken can drive me to the Apple Store once he gets home from work so one of the "Geniuses" can help me out. I'm sure all I need to do is buy some new files to get it up and running.

I just couldn't wait to tell you I read your first piece on www.huffingtonpost.com! I know you said this is just a day job for you since your goal is to be a novelist, but I thought it was fabulous! I'm very interested to hear more about how you got the idea to write about this topic. Had you always wondered which celebrities have the worst skin, or did your editor give you the assignment? Did you get to choose which celebrities you profiled, or is that something you will get the chance to do once you've been working there a little longer? Did you have to consult with a dermatologist for research? Whenever you get the chance to reply, I'd love to hear all the details!

I would also love to hear what the response has been to your work. Do you know if Arianna Huffington has had a chance to read the piece? I've always liked Arianna Huffington. A few weeks ago, I heard an interview with her on NPR, where she spoke very candidly about going through a divorce in the late 1990s with two young children. There was something very luminous about her that came through, even on the radio, though she was discussing a topic that I'm sure was very complicated for her. She seems like a very vibrant and fun-loving person. If I ever meet Arianna Huffington, I'll make sure to tell her about the Greek restaurant I worked at in college, Symposium. I bet she and I would have a lot in common!

With mountains and lakes of love,

Mom

PS—I hope it's okay that I showed Ken's roommate, Ron, your piece. He agrees with you about Cameron Diaz, though we both think she is still very pretty.

Your Hot Cousin Paul,
on the Fact That You Accidentally
Just Swiped Right on Each Other's Tinders

Ummmmmmmmm yeah so that happened.

I'm down in the den (0.0 miles away from your room, ha) watching *True Detective* if you want to join me.

Holidays, man.

Your Little Sister,
Whose Last Boyfriend Worked Part-Time
at a Tire Store,
Thinks Your Taste in Men Is Improving

U there????????

Ugh bitch stop leaving your FB open cause u get my hopes up!!!!!

I just wanted to let u know I stalked that dude Raj u are dating and HE IS SO FUCKIN HOT. def better than yr usual type of pastyass white dudes that look like homeless ppl.

Girl, get it.

Your Mom, Who Lives Alone in a Condo,
Is Extremely Excited about Your New Boyfriend

Hi honey,

I can't stop thinking about my visit to Los Angeles and that wonderful lunch we had with Raj last weekend. First of all, I thought the restaurant he found for us on Yelp.com was just fabulous. I'll definitely be telling my friend Yona, from temple, about it—she's planning a visit to LA soon to visit her daughter Elyse at Scripps College, where she's studying biology.

I also wanted to let you know that I figured out how to download Raj's album on iTunes, so you can disregard the messages I left you. I had to make a stop at Best Buy to pick up a new microwave, and they helped me figure it out. Please tell him I really enjoyed it! It was really evocative. Not just the lyrics—although I thought the line about waking up in Vegas after too much whiskey was very unique.

I also loved the way each song was infused with some subtle influences that felt distinct to his heritage. Even though Raj's music is in a very different genre, listening to his album reminded me of one of my favorite memories of being at Barnard—going to Greenwich Village with friends to hear Ravi Shankar perform in a darkened club. I hope it doesn't make you uncomfortable that I'm sharing this, but that was the night I tried magic mushrooms. I have such vivid memories of standing on the roof of a taxicab as it sped back uptown to the campus, hopping back and forth between various taxicabs as they stopped at red lights, just for fun.

In hindsight, I'm sure I was hallucinating and was actually inside the cab.

Anyway, please tell Raj he has a big fan in me—and not just because I'm your mother. I really do love all different styles of music. I remember during my year in Holland, I spent a lot of time listening to traditional Turkish music in a hookah bar down the block from where I was staying—just a couple blocks from the "Red Light District," which as you can imagine in those days was pretty wild!

Thinking back, I can't help but wonder how many of those women became afflicted with various sexually transmitted diseases—it was the sexual revolution, and we didn't know what we know now about AIDS, etc.

One more thing. I wanted to know, just for my own information: is "Raj" short for something? I know traditionally it means "king," and that name really seems to fit him! He has very elegant bone structure. There's something almost regal and timeless about it, like pictures I remember reading in the Ramayana in my religion survey course as an undergraduate. And his smile is very mischievous! It's almost like he just heard a secret he's dying to tell, but knows he can't. I see why you find him so intriguing.

Love,
Mom

Your Grandma Rose Has Some Questions about Your Interracial Relationship

Julie, Thank you for visiting me last week and introducing me to your friend. I appreciated that he held the door open for me when we went out for ice cream. Your mother just told me on the phone that he was Muslim. I thought he was just Indian. Does he know you're Jewish?

Try to tell him before too much time passes. In my experience, it's best to give people that information as soon as possible. What they do with it is up to them.

Your Dad, Who Asked Your Last Boyfriend If He Watches Porn, Is Wondering Why He Hasn't Met Your New Guy

Dear Julie,

While having a routine dental checkup this morning, I had my routine check-in with Dr. Leung about your love life (it seems your mother was recently fitted for a costly mouthguard—one wonders if this is the sort of "miscellaneous expense" to which my sizable alimony is directed). In any case, Dr. Leung mentioned you have a new love interest.

I wonder why you didn't share this happy news with your own father sooner. I remember fondly a time when you were more forthcoming in matters of the heart.

Speaking of intimacy, I read your latest online article regarding Jennifer Aniston and the rumor that all her close friends are on her payroll. Did I tell you that while in medical school, I diagnosed one of her uncles with a rare form of brain cancer, saving his life?

So it would seem that when it comes to the Anistons, one member of our family giveth, and the other taketh away.

Love,
Dad

Your New Boyfriend's Dog Has Some Words of Caution

Madam,

Please forgive my formality in addressing you thusly. We English bloodhounds are exceedingly well bred and hold the fairer sex in the highest esteem, never using a term so crude as "bitch" to refer to those who whelped us.

I trust you will agree that we have established a certain familiarity in the five months you have been engaged in a romantic relationship with my master. Night after night, I perch at the foot of Raj's bed as you two partake of the pleasures of the flesh, averting my noble gaze out of respect but unable to ignore the passion you share mere metres from where I lay my head. Your mutual relief in having found one another in this lonely metropolis called the City of Angels is truly heartening. After, as your twin heartbeats slow, I have solemnly absorbed intimate confessions of your deepest secrets: your adolescent body dysmorphia, your consuming anxiety concerning your mother's downward spiral in the wake of her divorce from your father, who may for his part be skipping his prescribed doses of lithium. Likewise, my master has allowed you to glimpse his innermost fear: will his independent rock band fail to transcend in a marketplace already so saturated with musical outfits that combine the instrumentation of nineteen-eighties synth pop with warmer, folk-inspired harmonies in the vein of Jeff Tweedy and Wilco? Never do I allow my eyelids—already so heavy, as is my breed's birthright—to close until you both have dozed off to sleep, his arms curled around your tiny frame, safe in his care as you enter a dream-scape of fantasies that this could last forever.

It is with a leaden heart that I must inform you that Raj would make a completely unsuitable partner for you in the long term.

I daresay, on the surface I understand his appeal as a companion. Raj's broad shoulders, commanding baritone, and impeccable taste in slim-fitting, subtly tattered cordu-roy blazers suggest erudition and refinement, the kind of man who is familiar with varietals of wine you have never even heard of, yet also understands the value of a sponta-neous road trip. In dreaming of a life together, one cannot help but envisage fireside cuddles on a couch in Vermont, a delightfully quirky wedding ceremony scored with original compositions by the groom himself, perhaps a trip to India to meet his extended family, during which you would surely convince his grandmother, whose dying wish is that he marry an Indian woman from their specific caste and village in Gujarat, that she may now rest in peace.

Although the nature of my relationship with Raj is admittedly distinct, I once imagined a version of such com-panionship myself: snowy walks in the woods, a naughty, secret nonverbal communiqué at dinner parties as he slips me scraps of roast chicken or tilapia under the table, a for-ever home in his lap. And indeed, in the year after he res-cued me, my master found me delightful, commemorating our newfound bond with photographs of me peacefully rest-ing across his knee, which he proudly shared with his entire online community.

As time wore on, however, Raj's true nature as a partner

revealed itself. Wholly unprepared was I for the callous brute who now checks his e-mail repeatedly when I need to be exercised, the tormentor who makes me wait hours for food as he scrolls endlessly through photographs of glorious meals posted by friends of friends he has only met once, the heartless cur who once became so intoxicated while watching a game of American football that he neglected to let me outside to relieve myself before he retired to his bedroom, leaving me no choice but to soil the living-room rug. I fear you are bound for a similar fate. However charming Raj may act in these first few months, these halcyon days filled with the food-truck festivals and Netflix marathons of early courtship, make no mistake: a life as his companion is one of constantly feeling inadequate, far less compelling than the games of virtual Scrabble he plays on the toilet. Sadder still would be to bring a child into this world together, only to find you have victimized an innocent at the hand of his punishing neglect. (I may be remiss in assuming this as a hazard; if so, forgive me. My species does not practice this so-called "pull-out method" to which you have resorted, at Raj's behest, in the bedroom.)

Lest you see these cautionary words as betokening some sort of aristocratic bias on my part, on the basis of Raj's heritage, I should mention that I myself am no stranger to hurtful profiling on the basis of race. Being one-eighth Afghan hound, I have encountered all manner of nasty assumptions in my lifetime, particularly in light of our global political situation. Nay, my concern for your fate is entirely humanistic, specific to my master himself and rooted in the pain of my own devastated dreams of an idyllic life together as man and beast.

SUSANNA FOGEL

Should you choose to heed my warning, I will surely miss your company; the two evenings I spent at your apartment while Raj attended his former roommate's bachelor party in Nevada remain two of the happiest in all my life. Never shall I forget our hours-long hike around the reservoir with your friend Jordana and her enchanting (if unfortunately proportioned) dachshund, nor your thought-provoking meditation on whether either of you would ever consider freezing your eggs. For whatever my opinion may be worth, I think this is an option worth considering as you await a partner who truly deserves you.

Yours in perpetuity,
Morrissey the bloodhound

Postscript—Despite my misgivings about you and my master as a suitable pair, rest assured that I have always approved of your preferred position for physical coupling. In the days before my neutering, that was my favorite style as well.

Your Grandma Rose Heard You Got Fucked Over

Julie, I got your message about your Indian friend. That's too bad. He was cute. Maybe you expect too much from these men. All you young people expect too much now. You kids talk about men like you're in a salad bar and you can just choose a scoop of everything you want on your plate and skip the coleslaw if you don't like coleslaw. The truth is a man is his own plate, and you just have to eat it even if it comes with coleslaw, which it always does.

Your Grandma Rose
Has a Slightly Different Take on Infidelity

Julie, I got your e-mail. I didn't know there was another woman in the picture with your Indian friend, but I still think your expectations are too high. Willie had girlfriends after we got married. When we were living in Italy, while he was a doctor for the air force, there was a young girl who came to clean the hospital at night. He started staying late most nights. I never learned her name, but I knew what was going on. I'm not stupid. But I got to live in Italy, so I figured as long as he doesn't knock her up . . . Luckily, we moved back to New York before that happened. Maybe luck isn't the right word, because the reason we left Italy was that we were Jewish and the Germans were starting to say some things we didn't like the sound of.

Your Dad, a Neurologist,
Has Some Advice about Your Writing Career

Dear Julie,
Have you ever heard of someone named Lena Dunham? She is significantly younger than you, but look her up. It may be useful to consider having a career like hers.

Dad

Your Sister Thinks a Road Trip to Visit Her Slutty Birth Mom Might Be Fun

Hey Babes!

First things first i saw the pix of elisa's wedding and you looked gorge. even tho her bridesmaids dresses were kind of ugly!!! and why did she make u guys wear those huge necklaces? wait you said Elisa designs jewelry now. OMG were those her creations??!?!?! no wonder she is struggling in her work life hahaha. shes really nice tho im glad she met a dude. i still remember the first time i met her when i came to visit u at college when i was like 11 and she got me stoned while u were at class and you got soooooo fuckin mad at her! little did u know id already been smoking weed for like two years AND stealing random pills from dads office whenever he got samples for work LOL. i love how dad was basically my dealer. shit that man is so lucky i didn't fuckin OD! like lock up your business dude there are innocent children in your house!

oh also was that guy sitting next to u in the pix your ex-boyfriend ben? that guy was soooo in love with u. OMG remember when u broke up and he left a basket of vitamins outside yr door with a love note that was all YOU NEVER GOT ENOUGH CALCIUM JULIE. so fuckin creepy. did he try to hit it again???

so more importantly . . . the reason i am writing u. you know how i told you i called the adoption agency and they gave me my mother's name? ummmmm ok its so weird to say my mother and not be talking about our crazy-ass mom. whatever u know who i mean. anyway i found the woman on FB and then i was out with my store manager getting happy hr and we got super fuckin trashed and i requested her and she approved me and i FB chatted her??? like um hi lady u don't know me but ummmmm remember that time u didn't use a condom with a dude u didn't even know? about that . . . haha.

but yah her name is kim and she seems nice actually. she said if i ever pass thru where she lives i should email her . . . and guess what? it turns out she lives in cali now. i guess she has her own salon in bakersfield wherever the fuck that is? so i was wondering if I drove up from AZ would you ever wanna go up there with me for the day to meet this random lady??? we cd even stay overnight at some cheap-ass motel and go do random shit in this town when we're done with coffee? i looked up bakersfield and theres like six gun ranges if u are interested in going shooting? lemme guess . . . you do NOT want to do that haha. maybe there is bowling or something more yr speed. i will look it up after i find a coffee shop to try and meet this lady at. the adoption website thingy I am on says go to a coffee shop with yr mother because its public and safe but like excuse me people but what could this lady do that is worse than abandoning a fuckin newborn baby?!

OMG maybe I should meet kim at the fuckin gun range haha. or maybe there is a coffee shop at the gun range hahahahaha.

so yah just let me know if u are interested. i would just need 3–4 days notice so i can request time off from my boss. he will def give it to me because he has been macking on me aaaaaaaall fuckin year. its like ok dude slow your roll! u are 40!!!! go pick on someone yr own age hahaha.

> Luv u to the moon + backkkkkkk
>
> jane

Ps—if i do end up passing thru yr hood can we go to the petersen automotive museum? is that near you? i wanna see where Biggie got shot.

Your Emotionally Withholding Dad Has Some More Career Advice

Julie,

I just read the article in the *New York Times Magazine* about the next generation of young female novelists. In case you missed it, there are interviews with dozens of women under thirty who already have lucrative book deals. Some have also already been nominated for (or won) prestigious literary awards.

It might be helpful to your career if you could get yourself featured in the *New York Times*.

> Dad

Your Mom's Rabbi Has a Great Idea for a TV Show!

Dear Julie,

My name is Josh Salz and I'm the new rabbi at Temple Emanuel. Your mother probably told you I would be contacting you about an idea I have for a TV show that I believe could be a huge hit.

So where do I start? Well, how about the beginning. When people think of rabbinical school, they probably picture bookish types who spend all their time thinking about the Torah. This could not be further from the truth. It's more like a prime-time soap opera with a constant stream of scandals, steamy love affairs, and bitter rivalries. I can't tell you the number of times I've been in the middle of telling someone a true story from my life and they stop me and tell me this could be on television. Unfortunately, I don't have time to focus on writing it because my work hours are very demanding and I have two sons in Junior High. It's a shame, because I took a creative writing class at Syracuse and I know I have the talent, but in life we make choices. That's exactly what my show is about . . .

The main characters:

RABBI JAKE is the older, wiser rabbi in his early forties who counsels all the students. He seems to have it all together, with a beautiful wife and two sons in Junior High. But the show will keep flashing back to when he was at the rabbinical school twenty years ago and learning these lessons for the first time. He was the resident heartbreaker on campus, and in flashbacks we will see him sleeping with all the hottest girls, including many who were not Jewish. Even now, most of his female students are attracted to him and are always turning his office hours into opportunities to try to have affairs with him. This will cause a lot of conflict in the show. There is also conflict with the rabbi's family, because his sons are both straight-A students and there is a lot of jealousy in the community about that. His older son, Max, got in the 99th percentile on his PSATs and was recruited by the Johns Hopkins gifted-student summer program. That could be an episode. And every episode of the show would start with Rabbi Jake delivering a sermon to his class. We can use my actual sermons for this part because they have a huge impact on people. I would love to bring that kind of emotion to millions of viewers every week who are sick and tired of the same old *CSI*. CASTING IDEAS: Clive Owen.

MIRIAM had always been daddy's little girl. But when she chose to enter the Yeshiva, her father stopped speaking to her because he is Orthodox and does not approve of female rabbis. Miriam reacted to this by spiraling out of control. She is the first person to try to have an affair with Rabbi Jake, and when he rejects her, she openly eats a ham-and-cheese sandwich in the middle of one of his lectures for revenge. She is wild and unpredictable ... and that's exactly what makes her so sexy. CASTING IDEAS: Zooey Deschanel (she just converted to Judaism and would be perfect for the part).

ELLIOTT was raised by liberal Jews who rarely went to temple. Then his parents died in one of the hijacked planes on 9/11, and Elliott turned to faith for answers.

Elliott is very shy and buttoned up, the "nice guy" who girls always like as just a friend. He will end up turning to Rabbi Jake to teach him his ways with women, and with Jake's help he eventually becomes the class Don Juan. But the one girl he wants, he can't have: Miriam, who only has eyes for Jake. CASTING IDEAS: Andrew Garfield (he's British but he can do the accent).

DAVID is the comic relief of the show. He is gay (training to be a reconstructionist rabbi), with crazy hair and style, but his options for dating are obviously limited at school. He always jokes that he is going to "turn" Rabbi Jake. We can always count on David to tell it like it is, even if it flies in the face of other people's expectations or the Torah. Casting ideas: The page from *30 Rock*.

And now, some episode ideas . . .

—Miriam steals a statue of Maimonides from the middle of campus (my ex-girlfriend actually did this) and holds it for ransom. The other characters have to convince her to bring it back before she gets expelled. Will Miriam really throw away her chance to be a rabbi just for some childish rebellion?

—Rabbi Jake convinces Elliott to go to therapy to finally deal with his parents' deaths, but Elliott starts having flashbacks (we can use actual footage of the 9/11 attacks) and ends up running away from campus. Everyone has to work together to find him. The final scene, which would be filmed in the Pentagon, will be incredibly powerful.

—David meets the perfect guy while shadowing Rabbi Jake at a bris. So what's the problem? The love of his life is the baby's father, and he's married to a woman! Oy vey! This would be more of a comedy episode. At one point they can get trapped in a coat closet together, which is obviously ironic. A title for this episode could be "In the Closet."

—A terrorist threat by a local branch of ISIS causes a lock-down at the school temple. Rabbi Jake must negotiate with the terrorists to free three of the hostages . . . David, Miriam, and Elliott. Rabbi Jake ends up outsmarting ISIS.

—A very special episode will take place in Cherry Hill, New Jersey. Rabbi Jake is flown in by a wealthy couple to officiate their daughter's bat mitzvah and ends up hanging out with Jay Z, who is performing at the party because the girl's father is his lawyer. This is actually something that happened to me, so I bet we could get Jay Z on the show. None of the other characters need to be in this one.

There are lot more ideas where that came from. This wouldn't be a lot of work for you because I have all the stories, I just need someone to write them down. Let's try to talk next week. My schedule is packed, but I'll make the time.

Rabbi Joshua Salz
Sent from my AdonaiPhone

Your Mom Needs Your Help
Picking Out a Cool CD

Hi sweetie,

I just found an e-mail in my "outbox" that I thought had been sent to you earlier in the week. It's possible my computer was broken that day. I'm going to make an appointment at the Apple Store to have them take a look at my computer so this doesn't happen again. I was writing you to ask if the new rabbi at my temple can contact you with an idea he has for a television show that sounds fabulous. I know you don't write for television, but I thought since you live in Hollywood you might have some friends who did and might be able to help him. Maybe he already reached out to you.

I can't wait to introduce you to Rabbi Josh the next time you're in town. He's a lot of fun. He has a wonderful sense of humor (he was the leader of an "improv" comedy troupe as an undergraduate at Syracuse) and he has a real passion for music and art. He's also very athletic. Back in New York, he was in a soccer league for rabbis and priests, and his team had a name that was just hysterical. I'm forgetting the name now, but it has something to do with gold stars. And I can tell he really appreciates me too—sometimes if I have a break between patients, I stop by the temple and we walk into Coolidge Corner to Panera Bread for lunch. He's married, but he never mentions his wife or seems like he is in any particular rush to get home at the end of the day, so there may be some trouble there.

Anyway, I need some help from my "guru" (that's you!). Next week is Rabbi Josh's birthday, and I would love to get him something special. As I said, he's a real music buff, and he has said in the past that he likes "alternative rock," so I would love to get him a CD. I went in to Newbury Comics on Needham Street yesterday and asked what kind of alternative rock they recommended, but they said it was a very big category and I got overwhelmed. Any recommendations? The other day he was playing music in his office by that band you like about the vampire weeks, so maybe something in that vein. Let me know if you have any ideas.

Before I sign off, I should tell you about a little plan Rabbi Josh and I are cooking up. I recently told him I never had a bat mitzvah, and he said at his old congregation, several of the adults had them later in life. Their whole families fly in from all over the country and they have a big party. Wouldn't that be fun? You and Jane could come home and stay for the week. My condo is a little too small for a party, but maybe we could rent out the back room at La Casa De Pedro in Watertown (the place with the great plantains you love). Can you imagine your mother "becoming a woman"?

Let me know about the CD!

Love,
Mom

Your Grandma Rose Is Sick of Her Friend's Sexual Bragging

Julie, Your mom came for dinner last night. She said she had a nice visit with you in California. But she showed me a picture of you. You're a bag of bones. I hope you aren't getting up to any funny business with your food like you used to. If you get too thin at your age it adds years to your face, and a man always prefers to lie on a soft mattress.

Your mom has been coming for dinner a lot. She says she doesn't want me to get lonely, but she's not fooling anyone about who's lonely. At least when she comes I don't have to eat with Maureen. Maureen tells the same story every night: she walked in on Walter changing in the bathroom after yoga and they horsed around in there. Big deal. She'll take her teeth out for anyone.

Your Dad, Who Lacks Boundaries, Wants to Talk about Your Body

Dear Julie,

I saw Dr. Leung for a cleaning this morning, and she mentioned you had broken up with your boyfriend, Raj. She mentioned a betrayal on his part and said you are having a very hard time with the loss.

You should check out the piece in today's *New York Times* about freezing your eggs, if you haven't already. There is nothing wrong with a nontraditional family.

I hope this makes you feel better.

Dad

SUSANNA FOGEL

Your Hot Cousin Paul
Doesn't Want Things to Be Awkward
at His Wedding

Hey Julie,

Thanks for your e-mail updating your RSVP to our wedding. Molly and I were sorry to hear about you and your boyfriend, but thanks for letting us know sooner rather than later so we had time to adjust the seating chart. Just so you know, we tried to seat you with one of your parents, but it's a little complicated because they both requested to sit on opposite ends of the banquet hall from one another. And my mom asked me to make sure there are an even number of people at all the tables in the middle of the room. Anyway, the options were limited.

The good news is that there's one empty seat at table 18 with all of Molly's sorority sisters from Indiana and their husbands who work in finance in the Midwest.

Also, I'm not sure if you were planning on giving a toast at the wedding—your speeches are always the highlight of family events—but in case you are thinking about it, I wanted to mention that Molly's family is pretty conservative. If you don't mind, please don't mention any of the stuff that happened in that outdoor shower on the Cape when we were kids, the time in college that my friends and I had interviews in the city and went to a party in your dorm and I fell asleep in your bed with you, or that random Tinder thing that happened a couple years ago that meant nothing to either of us because we aren't even attracted to each other at all and never have been because we're related and that wouldn't be right. I just don't know how the Petersons would take it, and I want everything to go smoothly as Molly and I start our life together.

Thanks for understanding. And again, we were sorry to hear about you and your boyfriend.

Paul

Your Sister, Who Didn't Pay Her Taxes Last Year, Was Wondering If She Can Crash with You

hi babe i cant believe im seein u in one week! i totally forgot about pauls wedding til like five minutes ago and aunt andrea sent me this email like ummmm so are u coming to my sons wedding lol. i was like, oh weird i put my rsvp in the mail I wonder what happened to it! then she didn't say anything, she was just quiet like she is whenever she is mentally judging . . . aka ALWAYS . . .

and now brandon (bf) is pissed at me cause we were supposed to go camping this weekend and he borrowed his brothers Rav4. oh well brandon can suck it cause I GET TO SEE MY SISTAAAAAAA sorry i just had two mochas. ugh paul said he put me at a table with dad for the dinner part so I guess I can look forward to seeing lots of pix of his baby/our new brother (??????). WTF is a 60 year old man gonna do with a fuckin toddler? They'll both be chillin in diapers lol.

also sorry to have to ask but is it cool if i sleep in your hotel room? i figured theres space cause raj isn't coming anymore (btw i unfollowed him on social media but i can refollow him if you want me to keep u updated on how much he sucks). anyway i tried to get a room on hotwire but like everything is sold out at this point and im not really trying to spend half my paycheck on a room at some country club.

btw why is paul getting married at a fuckin golf course? im sure it was her idea—i looked her up on FB and all her pix are like her playing tennis in an all white tennis outfit (????). i better not show her any pix of brandon cause she probably hates mexicans and hes half mex haha. omg hes so fuckin hot you have to meet him.

but yah lemme know about the room. also brandon has a friend in Virginia who said he can meet me at the airport with edibles so you will be glad you said yesssssss ☺

jane

Ps—did i tell you I got fuckin pulled over on my way to work for playing my music too loud?!!!!! the cop goes, this is a residential street not a nightclub. bahahaha

Your Dad's Six-Year-Old Son from His Second Marriage Discusses His Superior Childhood

Dear half sister,

I just wanted to shoot you a friendly reminder that Tuesday is Dad's birthday. I know I've only been alive for his past six and you've been around for twenty-three more than that, but I've noticed a pattern where you call a week late, claiming you just found a text that you thought you sent on his birthday trapped in your outbox. I hope it's not too brazen of me, given my relative youth, to call bullshit on that. (I'd like to also take this opportunity to express my gratitude for the fact, given Dad's advanced age when I was conceived, that I have any mental acuity at all!) Anyway, just figured I'd help you get out ahead of it this year.

So, what's new? How goes the job search? How was your weekend? I've had a relaxing one, just lounging on the couch with some cartoons. I'm guessing that's how you spent much of your childhood too, though from what I understand, yours was a brown corduroy sleeper with cigarette burns on the arms that Dad found at a yard sale in East Palo Alto when he and your mother were living paycheck to paycheck. This one's an original Baughman. Dad's really gotten into midcentury modern design now that he has disposable income.

I know what you're thinking: his newfound aesthetic appreciation must have made Dad even *more* uptight, right? Luckily, it's the opposite. Last year, during a bout of stomach flu, I threw up on one of the cushions. I was terrified he'd be furious—having heard tales of his explosive temper during your youth—but he just laughed it off. Dad says he's much more able to put things in perspective now. The yoga helps, as do retirement and the fact that he's finally found true love with my mom. No offense to your mother, obviously. She seems like a lovely woman, if Facebook is any indication. And it sounds like Dad was pretty different back then too. (Lithium's a hell of a drug.)

SUSANNA FOGEL

Which is not to say he's never in a bad mood anymore; the man's only human. Last week he was downright miffed when I coated my noodles with what he regarded as a wasteful amount of truffle oil. Men and their artisanal extracts! Still, you can't help but be charmed by how much Dad's come to appreciate the finer things in life now that he's in the twilight of his. I'm certainly enjoying the spoils. I'd say my twos were significantly less terrible thanks to his housemade teething toast slathered with slow-cooked rabbit-hock puree and basil jelly. Is it true that when you were growing up and he was at the hospital until all hours doing his residency, he prepared your meals with something called a "microwave"? I can't say I've ever seen one up close. Dad got rid of ours before I was born, in light of recent studies about how they cause cancer. I'm sure he would have done the same for you if anyone back then had known what we know now. Have you heard about those advanced full-body scans you can get? I know they're expensive, and I don't know what your health care situation is, but we can certainly help you out if need be. How terrifying is cancer? Thank God by the time I'm your age, there'll probably be a cure.

Okay, I should probably wrap this up. Dad's calling me to join him for a walk in the woods. We're going to collect autumn leaves, then write prose poems. He's going through this whole Auden phase now that he finally has time for pleasure reading. I'm sure he'll tell you all about it when you call him on Tuesday (nudge, nudge). I hope you won't take me reaching out like this the wrong way. I'm sure that when I'm a grownup, I'll be just as busy and will forget to call home too. Of course, by then, Dad will probably be blind or deaf and won't register it enough to hold it against me. In any case, we're all really looking forward to seeing you at Passover.

Affectionately,
your half brother
Stuart Feller, age six

Your Mom Is Grateful
That You Made Her Look Cool

Hi sweetheart,
Rabbi Josh really liked the "Television on the Radio" CD you recommended!
    Thanks again for your help.

Love,
Mom

Your Dad's Friend
Who Makes You a Little Uncomfortable
Has Been Keeping Up with Your Life on Facebook

Julie—
Hey there, stranger.
    I just got home to Nantucket after spending a weekend with your dad and his family. I was up in Cambridge receiving an award from the *New England Journal of Medicine*

(they recently published my research on some hidden side effects of Accutane that I was the first to detect—you may have seen it retweeted last week by Dr. Oz). He and Mei-Ling seem well, as does Stuart. They promised to visit me in Hawaii on their way to see Mei-Ling's parents in Shanghai next summer.

I'm sure your dad mentioned this to you, but I just bought a condo on the Big Island.

I know you're probably sitting there scratching your head—after all, I'm such an East Coast guy, between my addiction to the symphony (know any good support groups for that?), all the lectures I attend just for fun, and my subscription to *The Atlantic*. But lately I've seen so many people I care about migrate west, including my daughter, Alicia, whose wife just got a job at Microsoft in Seattle. But I'm assuming you knew that already—I see you girls are Facebook friends. Love the new profile picture, by the way—has anyone ever told you that you bear a resemblance to Anna Karina (Godard's muse)?

Anyway, I know I made you this offer several years ago with my Nantucket digs, but if you ever find yourself planning a trip to Hawaii—perhaps for a reporting assignment?—why not save your travel stipend and stay with me? The guest bedroom has a California king bed and its own bathroom with floors made from polished rock imported from American Samoa (an island that also holds a special place in my heart—I spent a year there during med school, studying the impact of sun damage on the indigenous peoples). Also, the building itself is very safe. My unit overlooks a plein air market where the natives sell some beautiful shell jewelry that would look great with the dress you're wearing in your profile picture. Last but not least, The Spa at Kona Beach Hotel is just down the road. I'd be happy to hook you up with my favorite masseuse there, Nalani, who practices both Shiatsu and Swedish techniques. She always teases me for insisting that she talk me through everything she's doing so I can learn how to give as well as receive. That's just the kind of guy I am.

Needless to say, I'd be willing to bet money that if you came out to the island, you'd leave with a first draft of your novel. I'm biased, but it's been said that nothing stirs the artist's heart like a Pacific sunset—and the farther out you are in the Pacific, the more inspiring. Especially with a homemade daiquiri in your hand—Alicia and Maggie just bought me a margarita machine as a housewarming gift, and I've learned to do things with a pineapple that might just inspire you to switch from fiction writing to poetry.

Maybe sometime soon, you'll give me a chance to put those skills to the test.

Fondly,
Larry Shepherd

PS—Have you ever been swimming with sharks? Not in the Hollywood sense—I'm sure you do that on a daily basis—but literally? If you decide you'd like to come visit Hawaii and can give me a couple of weeks' notice, I can arrange a private under-water tour—for both of us, if you'd like a companion, or if you'd like to go alone with the guide, we could meet up afterward on the pier and watch the sunsets I mentioned.

SUSANNA FOGEL

PPS—I was just about to hit "Send" when I noticed you had posted your latest piece, "Celebs You Didn't Know Were in Mensa." I really had no idea about David Beckham.

Your Father, Who Is Probably on the Spectrum, Has a New Hobby

Julie,
Mei-Ling and I have been getting into writing haiku lately. I wanted to share the latest with you.

> *Autumn of my life*
> *At last, a son beside me*
> *Hours skipping stones*

I guess you're not the only writer in the family,

Dad

Your Late Grandfather, a Decorated Naval Officer, Is Wondering What Happened to Manhood

Heya Dumbo,
Remember I used to call you that 'cause you had the biggest goddamned ears? You used to cry like a little baby, but I know deep down you thought your Grandpa Dan was funny. My dad and grandpa always let me have it, and look at me; I turned out fine. Your mother used to nag me to

respect your feelings. I told her, lady, we're talking about someone who is two feet tall and shits her pants. I was in fucking Normandy. Respect is something you earn. Why does everyone have to be so goddamned sensitive? Ah, shit. Doesn't matter now—now that I'm dead and you grew into your big Dumbo ears.

Want to know how I know you grew into your ears? I watch you. Not like I'm some angel up in heaven; all that angel stuff's just a dumb myth for Jesus-freak retards anyway. Shit, people don't say "retard" anymore where you are, do they? No one has any fucking fun anymore. Anyway, once you die you get your own TV set. Each channel plays a person over there who's still alive. So I watch your channel sometimes. I always tune in on your birthday, just to see what you're getting up to. What have I learned? I'll say this—my little Dumbo can drink. But don't worry, I'm not a goddamned pervert—I change the station right before you let some asshole that doesn't deserve to lick the heel of your boot take you home to bed. Seems like that happens most years. I did like that Indian kid 'til he went off with that dumb ginger with the big tits. Don't worry—he's cheating on her now too.

Here's the problem with men today: they're not. That's the problem. You better hope there's not another world war, 'cause if there's a goddamned draft and those pussies ship off we can kiss our great nation goodbye. Only time I see a real man over there now is when I tune into a channel in goddamned Arabia and watch those fundamental boys blowing up pizza joints. At least they have conviction. Your little friends with their goddamned computer diaries about where

SUSANNA FOGEL

to find the best soup dumplings on the East Side may as well put rollers in their hair like my great aunt Violet, who always smelled like dill pickles. I run into her over here sometimes. She still smells like goddamned pickles.

The worst was that stupid kid you were seeing back in New York—the one who was studying to be an expert on goddamned coffee. Yeah, he was a real piece of shit. What the fuck is a "vegan," anyway? Never mind a steak—what kind of man with two nuts won't even eat a goddamned egg? No granddaughter of mine is gonna marry a man she can share pants with, even if I have to rise from the dead to stop it myself. No wonder he couldn't fuck, either.

You know that time Grandma and I came to watch you when you were little and your folks went to the beach for the weekend? First off, they should've sprung for a room with a better view; maybe then they wouldn't have split. See? I told you your grandpa was funny. Anyway, I still remember we walked in on you in that tent in the backyard. You were playing with that boy from the neighborhood, showing each other your parts. Caught with your pants down. Let me tell you, *that* kid was a real man. Go look him up.

I gotta go, Dumbo—dinner time over here. Tell your pussy little coffee friend from New York that whatever I eat, I'm killing it with my bare hands.

Grandpa Dan

Your Mom Has Some Thoughts on This Year's Holiday Releases

Hi honey,

I know you're very busy at work getting ready for the holidays and I'm sure that's why you haven't returned my call, so I am using e-mail because it seems "lower key" than calling again. I always get a little sentimental this time of year, when everyone comes home to see their families, even though we don't really do that since we don't celebrate Christmas. Of course, if you felt like making the trip this year, I would be happy to pay for half of your ticket, but no pressure. I don't feel lonely, especially since I made friends with a woman who just moved in across the hall. Did I tell you about Loni? We discovered we both love movies, so we've been seeing a film almost every day. I'm sure you don't have a lot of time to see movies, so I thought I would send you my "reviews" of the newest releases to help you figure out which ones are worth your time.

MARTIANS—BEST MOVIE OF THE YEAR!!!!!! Matt Damon is incredibly lovable and resourceful. And understanding—even though his friends assumed he was dead and stranded him in space, he never blames them. He is exactly the kind of man I would love to see you end up with, someone patient and forgiving who could take care of you even in the most dangerous of circumstances (like if the drought in California really does lead to a shortage of bees and our planet is deprived of oxygen—I forwarded you that article last week). I know you say dating in California is tough, but I've met several single men your age here in

SUSANNA FOGEL

Boston recently who remind me a lot of Matt Damon in *Martians*. If you do end up coming home this month, I can introduce you. They would have to stay here in town for their jobs, but I explained that you're a writer, so you can potentially be flexible.

BRIDGE OF SPIES—This was the movie I had been most excited to see because Tom Hanks is my favorite actor and, as you know, I came of age during the Cold War. But I have to admit I was very confused because, without giving too much away, there was only one spy on the bridge. At least, I only counted one. I did doze off for a bit in the middle because the film is very long and I haven't been sleeping well lately. Loni thinks this might be a thyroid issue, but I don't want you to worry. The next time you're in town, maybe you can take me to the doctor because Loni said her uncle died of a thyroid issue that went undiagnosed, but I know how busy you are, so just let me know if anything opens up in your schedule. Anyway, back to the film—it's possible other spies came and went while I was asleep.

JAMES BOND MOVIE—I didn't particularly care for the film, but I will see anything with Daniel Craig. I'm not sure if you knew this, but he's married to Rachel Wise (sp?) and helping her raise her child from her first marriage. A few months ago, I saw a photograph of them walking out of a temple in London on Rosh Hashanah. He seems incredibly respectful of her family's traditions. I would love to see her act in more films!

BURNT—All the food looked delicious, but I don't find Bradley Cooper likable. He just always seems like he's up to no good.

THE DANISH GIRL—An incredibly powerful film starring the boy who played Stephen Hawking. Once again, he completely transforms, this time into a woman who is transgendered. Did I mention I have a new friend at Health-works (my gym) who used to be a man? I've told her all about you. If you do end up visiting at the holidays, maybe we can all go to yoga together. Talking to her might spark some ideas for your writing. I know you said you've been blocked lately.

ROOM—I should warn you that this film has a very disturbing concept: The story is about a young woman who was kidnapped and locked in a shed, where she is sexually abused by her kidnapper. His abuse produced a young child, whom she has been raising alone for years. At first I found this incredibly upsetting, but then I realized the entire plot is actually just a metaphor. It represents the powerful bond between a mother and child and how many sacrifices a mother makes. I related deeply, remembering how it felt to hold you in my arms as an infant, feeling like nothing would ever come between us. When the mother and son even-tually escape from the shed, I found myself getting incredi-bly sad because I knew the strength of their bond would be compromised forever and all the mother's sacrifices would be forgotten.

JOY—This film isn't out in theaters yet, but I already have my ticket! You may have heard they filmed the whole thing around here. Angie, the receptionist at Healthworks, got to be an extra when they filmed a scene near her house. She said there was a lot of waiting around, but she got to meet Jennifer Lawrence, who was very nice and even offered Angie a piece of her gum. We're all going to see the movie together on opening night to support Jennifer Lawrence.

THE REVENANT—Another one I haven't seen, but I watched the preview and I've seen enough. I don't like the message—according to the reviews, Leonardo DiCaprio's friends abandoned him after assuming he died, which is very similar to the premise of *Martians*. But unlike that film, where everyone works together to save Matt Damon, this film focuses on revenge and violence. I would prefer everyone just dealt with the issue the way they did in *Martians*.

HARFA KOZY—I'm not sure if this is playing where you are, but this is a wonderful independent Polish film Loni and I saw at the Museum of Fine Arts. The story is about a young orphan girl who lives with her uncle in a shack and spends her whole life dreaming of playing the harp in the Warsaw Philharmonic. Unfortunately, her family is too poor to afford instruments, but when she turns ten, her uncle makes her a harp from the bones of her pet goat. It's a wonderful film about the power of family and music, and it ends with some wonderful singing and dancing. The title translates to "Harp Goat." I highly recommend it.

SPOTLIGHT—An incredibly powerful exploration of how only a Jewish man could bring change to a corrupt system.

Okay, it's getting late here, so I'd better hit the hay. Just so you know, I would see any of these films again if you decided you were interested in coming home. Loni will be visiting her daughter in Chicago, so she won't be in town to go to movies with, but no pressure. I can always just bring my notebook to the theater and take notes for more "reviews," and that's all the company I need.

Love,
Mom

PS—It looks like my bat mitzvah will be taking place in April or May, which will give me plenty of time to learn my Torah portion without compromising my time and commitment to my analytic patients. I'm very grateful I have such a full life!

Your Sister,
Who Is Sleeping with Her Supervisor
at T. J. Maxx,
Needs a Favor

Um. Hi. First of all can we talk about mom having a bat mitzvah please!????? WHAT THE FUCK

i think shes just creepin on her new rabbi lol. i found him on FB and one of his pix is him with no shirt on!!!!

also . . . ok this is awkward but I have a little situation on my hands. remember that guy tyler from my work i was dating when you visited me? the 42 yr old who was still seeing someone he went to HS with and he was gonna break up with her but he felt bad cause he was kinda like a father to her kids? well speaking of fathers . . . i am kinda 6 weeks pregnant. of course i found out after i dumped him cause he was lying to me about a bunch of shit ☹ anyway i'm not trying to be a single mother on welfare right now so i think i just need to take care of it. is there any way u could lend me money and come with me to do it when we are both home for moms thing?

ok let me know and please dont tell mom or she'll talk about it in her bat mitzvah speech—haha not really but that lady does tell the world everything.

I LOVE YOU!!!!!!

jane

Your Dad
Just Heard about
His Ex-Wife's Adult Bat Mitzvah

Julie,

While having a cavity filled today, I heard from Dr. Leung that your mother will be having a bat mitzvah next month. Please pass along my congratulations, although I have to admit I was a little offended that she didn't think to send me an invitation.

In any case, I trust you'll keep me abreast of what she selects for her Torah portion. It would certainly be ironic if she chose a passage about Joseph, whose story, if you recall, centers on forgiveness. Hey, if the guy could forgive his brothers for selling him into slavery, one would think your mom could have pardoned a few bad investments on my part and not hired such an aggressive, bloodthirsty divorce lawyer who did obliterative damage to my finances.

Regardless, I hope the experience is spiritually rewarding

for her and brings you ample fodder for your comedic writings.

Love,
Dad

YOUR MOM JUST WANTS TO APOLOGIZE ABOUT THE CAPS LOCK

HI HONEY,
SORRY ABOUT THE CAPS LOCK! THE BUTTON IS STUCK, AND I CANT GET THAT LITTLE GREEN LIGHT TO GO OFF.

HOW ARE YOU DOING, SWEETIE? I JUST HAD A GREAT NIGHT IN WITH LONI. SHE JUST LEFT MY APARTMENT AND WENT ACROSS THE HALL TO HER APARTMENT, BUT I'M NOT TIRED YET. TONIGHT WE HAD OUR OWN LITTLE "WINE TASTING" WITH THREE DIFFERENT WINES WE BOUGHT AT WHOLE FOODS. LONI AND I ARE ON A MISSION TO PICK THE PERFECT WINE TO SERVE AT MY BAT MITZVAH NEXT MONTH. SHE ALSO INTRODUCED ME TO A WONDERFUL PHONE APPLICATION CALLED "SPOTIFY." YOU CAN LOOK UP ANY SONG YOU WANT AND CRE-ATE YOUR OWN PERSONAL PLAYLIST. THE SKY'S THE LIMIT! WE HAD A LOT OF FUN SINGING ALONG TO ARETHA FRANKLIN.

I CAN'T WAIT TO SEE YOU AND JANE NEXT MONTH AT MY BAT MITZVAH. I'M NERVOUS

SUSANNA FOGEL

ABOUT MY TORAH PORTION, BUT I KNOW ALL I HAVE TO DO IS LOOK OUT INTO THE CROWD AND FIND "MY GIRLS" AND I WON'T BE NERVOUS ANYMORE. AND DEBORAH IS GOING TO HELP ME WITH THE CANDLE LIGHTING. I FEEL MUCH CLOSER TO LONI THESE DAYS BUT DEBORAH IS ONE OF MY OLDEST FRIENDS SO IT SEEMED TO FIT THE THEME OF TRADITIONS.

ALSO, SPEAKING OF DEBORAH AND RACHEL, I DON'T KNOW IF YOU WERE HOPING TO SPEND TIME WITH RACHEL THAT WEEKEND, BUT JUST SO YOU KNOW, SHE E-MAILED ME TO ASK IF SHE COULD BRING HER NEW BOYFRIEND AND I SAID OF COURSE THAT WOULD BE FINE. SO I JUST WANTED TO LET YOU KNOW THAT SHE MAY NOT HAVE A LOT OF FREE TIME. IF YOU WOULD LIKE TO BRING A FRIEND, JUST LET ME KNOW. ANYONE IS WELCOME!

I ALSO INVITED LONI'S SON CRAIG. HE LIVES IN CHICAGO, SO HE'S NOT SURE IF HE CAN MAKE IT, BUT WE ARE CROSSING OUR FINGERS. CRAIG IS VERY HANDSOME. HE'S A FEW YEARS OLDER THAN YOU AND HE'S STILL GOING THROUGH A DIVORCE, BUT LONI THINKS THAT WILL BE FINALIZED WITHIN THE YEAR, SO WE WERE JUST PUTTING OUR HEADS TOGETHER.

LOVE,
MOM

Your Mom's Brother,
Who's Obsessed with Disney,
Has Been Looking at Tits

Jules and Jane,

I'm so sorry for the delay in scanning/sending you the photos for your mom's bat mitzvah slideshow. I was looking through all our old albums from our childhood and teen years, and honestly, I found very few where your mom has her shirt on! She was quite the little exhibitionist well into her teens . . . and while her spunk is part of her charm, I'm just not sure she'd want that advertised in a place of worship! What do you guys think?

> Hugs from Denver,
> Uncle Ken

PS—Just got a yarmulke custom-made with all the characters from *Aladdin*.

Your Grandma Rose
Just Got Back from the Casino

Julie, I just got back from Atlantic City. They took all of us oldies on the bus. I beat everyone at pool because when Willie and I were in Milan, all the doctors' wives got together to play. I won two thousand dollars in cash. Big deal—what is money to someone my age? I can't buy a new body. I can't pay to bring Dan back. I'm too old to go back to Italy. Everything I want is not on the market. I threw the bills out the window of the bus. The doctor here says I'm depressed. He's an idiot. I have to send this e-mail now and go down to the activity room for movie night. We are watching something starring Angelina Jolie, about a woman who breaks into other people's coffins. I don't care for her, so I may turn off my hearing aid.

Your Stepmother Has Some Theories about Why You're Still Single

Dear Julie,

Hi, it's Mei-Ling, your stepmother. Your father has no awareness of me writing, but as wife I bear burdens of his sorrows and aim to ameliorate concerns. Most recently, he expressed a worry for how your life will end romantically as it has been over one year since you have dated Raj and shortly you will be thirty. On this problem I have thought greatly and a variety of ideas are on my mind.

Firsthand, I think strongly that your style of dress is too pragmatic. In your last visit, upon meeting to eat family brunch at Einstein Bros. Bagels, I saw your loose pants and vest of corduroy purchased in boys department of H&M. In China this is unheard except in emergency where girl must pretend she has male identity to escape perilous ordeal. Your father wonders if you are in fact lesbian, but I have told him no woman is true lesbian. Lesbian is merely woman who has not met Mr. Right. Such is the reason we have no lesbian in China, where population heavily favors man, making it the case that no woman is left wanting.

I wish to contribute to solution of the problem with three gifts enclosed in this box. Three silk gowns. Beautiful and elegant, they were designed by Filene's Basement. Regarding your size I was unsure, as your father spoke of your recent coffee together in California during his big trip to meet the pharmaceuticals corporation in Sandiego. There, he observed you had gained weight. Nevertheless, to hang these garments upon your closet will surely provide inspiration for health and beauty in the New Year. Yet still better is to wear silks to holiday parties, to show suitors you are princess, not just freelance contributor to news website.

Beyond dress, I have noticed another thing problematic in your encounters with men. I noticed this as you brought home Raj for thanks giving two years back. After dinner as we were sitting fireside and your father discussed with Raj American presidents such as Ted Roosevelt, Raj was mistaken on one fact. You offered him the correction. Such shaming is not tolerable for man. It is often necessary to allow man to know most, although you may be the wiser, otherwise you castrate man and he thinks you are warrior, not wife. At the end of days, it is not about American presidents but about your own reign. My grandfather Fa stated, "If you stand on top of mountain, no man will pick flower." (In Mandarin, this rhymes.) You climbed to top of mountain as Raj stood at base of hill with peasantry. For this, he later acted in bad faith with sexy local bartender. Heartbreak resulted.

On the contrary, I will example one successful case that is your father and myself. In first dating, I overheard him

SUSANNA FOGEL

make multiple errors on topic of European debt crisis. Yet I remained silent and allowed him excessive height on mountain peak as I crouched in reeds below. In so doing, I prevailed and since then have no shortage of victories large and small. For example, upon meeting me your father had already surpassed the Middle Ages and remarked he did not want new wives or children. Yet I persuaded him through softness and gentle touch. Now I am due to bear a child in seven months, as he more than likely told you.

Yours truly,
Mei-Ling Feller

Your Dad, Who Represses Emotion, Is Feeling a Little Sentimental Today

Julie,
A special haiku I wrote in honor of your upcoming thirtieth birthday:

> *Child no longer*
> *Specter of my former life*
> *Still, sometimes she charms*

It's nice to see you aging gracefully. A handmade gift from Mei-Ling is in the mail.

Dad

Your iPhone Is Having Some Issues
with Your Relationship

Hey you,

Sorry it's taken me a minute to check in. I know I suddenly shut down on you yesterday. I'm just really bad with confrontation and I needed some time to think.

Okay . . . there's no easy way to say this, so I'll just rip off the Band-Aid. I've been thinking for a while now that our relationship has become kind of toxic. This isn't just about what happened yesterday when you dropped me in the toilet because you couldn't leave my side for three minutes, though that was a wake-up call. I've spent the last twenty-four hours in this bag of rice reflecting on how we got to this unhealthy place.

Honestly? Maybe we moved too fast when we first synched up.

I am not blaming you for that. I was right there with you. I mean, the beginning of any relationship is magical. It's not exaggerating to say I had never been turned on before I met you. And you'd never gone for a phone quite as smart as me. It was like a whole new world, a breath of fresh air after your two years with the Android Who Shall Remain Unnamed.

But then, I don't know. It just started to feel like you needed me too much. You had to check in every second—e-mail, Facebook, Instagram, Twitter. You always had to know the status of everything all the time. I felt like we could never just sit there comfortably on silent, recharging. I'm not sure how much you know about introverts, or cell

SUSANNA FOGEL

phones, but that's just how we're wired. If we don't fully recharge each time, eventually we just get drained—like, permanently.

Not that this is just about me. If you look inside yourself, you have to admit this hasn't been healthy for you either.

First, there's all the texting and driving. In the beginning, I got it. That's just what the honeymoon phase is: you want to be touching all the time, and the idea of getting caught only adds to the excitement. How fast can you turn me on at a stoplight before it turns green? Can you refresh me to completion without anyone seeing us? It was insanely hot at first. But after a while, once the novelty wears off, it's just like . . . do we really have to do this here? There's a time and a place for us to connect, you know?

To be honest, sometimes I felt like it wasn't even about me. It always seemed like you were kinda using me to make your ex jealous. All those times we'd take a picture together and it felt like we were just present, capturing a special moment together . . . and then you'd go on Instagram and post it because Raj still follows you. And do you think I didn't notice that whenever you'd log into Facebook, you'd check his page and cross-reference the pages of any women that commented on his posts? I know you say you're over that guy and it's been more than a year, but if that were true, you'd be setting more boundaries—and respecting mine.

Oh, and there's one more thing that's just felt a little off to me about us. This may seem small to you, but it's a big deal to me.

I'm really into film—like, classic cinema.

Whenever you'd use me to watch something shot in

35- or 70-millimeter anamorphic, I felt like I was helping you conduct this assault on the art form or something. Like, if Stanley Kubrick thought people would be watching his work on a two-by-three-inch screen, I sort of doubt he would have bothered making *2001*. Not that that's what we were watching. Maybe the director of *The Back-up Plan* doesn't mind.

Anyway, I think for both our sakes we should just move on. I know it'll be hard, but the sooner you can accept that, the sooner you can get back out there to the Apple Store and find a phone that can give you everything you're looking for.

And hey, even though I know this is the right thing for both of us, I'll always remember you and the memories we shared . . . like that amazing secret pic we took on the subway of that woman's entirely exposed butt crack. What was she thinking? I'm glad you synched that to your computer.

Take care, kiddo.

iPhone 4S

Your Dad Has Decided to Put You in the Middle

Dear Julie,

The next time you speak with your mother, please ask her to edit the settings on her e-mail account's spam blocker. I reached out to her recently and did not receive a reply; given the content, my only reasonable conclusion is that the missive did not reach her due to a hyperactive spam filter.

A common pitfall for those who stubbornly insist on maintaining an AOL address.

To bring you up to speed, I had contacted her regarding a disturbing diagnosis I received during a routine physical last week. There is a small blemish on my liver that will need to be removed exigently to prevent further health complications. Needless to say, this is rather ironic for a man who always limited his drinking, even as an undergraduate. Which is not to say I didn't have my fair share of youthful delusions about mortality—I just preferred more stimulating substances. If anything, I would have expected some delayed neurological damage from the LSD.

In any case, the medical procedure for my condition is very costly and not entirely covered by insurance—despite the laudable efforts of President Obama.

Unfortunately, my alimony payments to my ex-wife remain astronomical. In my letter to your mother, I suggested that I have more than compensated her for any heartbreak I may have caused her during the 1980s and 1990s and requested she forfeit all future payments so I can get my medical affairs in order. I then concluded my e-mail with an original haiku I composed specifically for her on the topic of bygone love.

No response for a week. As I say, I have chosen to give her the benefit of the doubt and write this off as a technological glitch. That said, another possible scenario is that your mother received the letter but failed to understand the gravity of my medical situation because her education is limited to a PhD.

Any help you could offer would be appreciated.

How are things on the home front? Especially in light

of this health scare, I can't help but find myself wondering if I will live to meet my grandchildren.

Love,
Dad

Your Sister Regrets Talking So Much Shit about Your Dad

Jules,
Tried to call u back but I think yr phone is dead. U need a new fuckin phone.

Dude Im kinda freakin out. Dad has been emailing me a lot of random shit which is just freakin me out bc I am not used to hearing from him unless he is telling me I should go to college or sending me random haikus about adoption (I told u about that right?). Also in his last email he attached a pic of him and me when I was a baby and he took me to the beach in this weird bonnet that looks like its from olden times??? I didn't know he kept pix of us . . .

But no it made me feel bad b/c all I do is bag on him . . . Not saying I brought a curse on his head or anything but I was just thinking like what happens if the surgery gets fucked up? As u know, that man and I have had our difficulties but if he died now that wd be fucking sad.

And what wd happen to his family? I wd kinda worry about Stuart! Like can that woman take care of a little kid by herself? Does she even have a drivers license?!!! Or would we have to like move in with her?

Ugh mom would be so excited we were moving back

SUSANNA FOGEL

to Boston she would shit herself. Hopefully this will not happen . . .

xx
Jane

Your Grandma Rose Has Thoughts about Your Dad's Negotiating

Julie, I heard what your dad's getting up to with your mom's money. Even if he's on his deathbed, she should not give him a dime. I know she played her part, but he was a perfectly rotten husband and now she's too old to find anyone else decent. That's just the fate of a woman. It's a sadness. Anyway, as far as I'm concerned your dad and his new family can go live in a hut made out of cow crap.

Your Dad, the Most Jewish Person You Know, Is Having a Come-to-Jesus Moment

Dear Julie,

My surgery is in two hours. Though I am optimistic that everything will run smoothly, I find myself compelled to reflect on my life and relationships with my loved ones. I hope you will forgive the cliché.

I figured e-mail was the optimal mode of communication, so you will have an electronic document you can easily refer back to as needed throughout your life.

It has been a treat to watch you grow from an irrepressible

little girl with a vibrant imagination into a creative, independent woman. I am pleased to see you pursuing the career path that always seemed to be your destiny. I remember your earliest works as a writer, when as a preteen you would sneak out of bed and crouch at the top of the stairs with a notebook, feverishly recording every word the "grown-ups" were saying down in the kitchen and adding your own colorful dialogue and scenarios. You would then perform it for us in the kitchen the next day as part of a series of skits you called "The After-Bedtime Truth"! I still remember how funny those were. I hope I live to see your work as a writer pay dividends—it can be painful to watch you spend your days behind a desk at a job that only nominally involves creativity—but if I am not so lucky, just know I believe it will.

(Unless, of course, you decide you are fulfilled by writing two-hundred-word blurbs on topics like Taylor Swift's revolving door of suitors, in which case I will attempt to withhold judgment from beyond the grave.)

As for companionship, I believe you will find that too—though if I may offer a suggestion, this may require you to be more open-minded about who Mr. Right might be. I speak from experience—I never thought the love of my life would be a woman who requires me to eat with chopsticks. It turns out the food is no less nourishing.

Finally, I should clarify something: I know before I was properly diagnosed and medicated for my illness, I was an erratic and unstable presence in your life. The reason I don't discuss this time often is not because I don't remember it—quite the opposite. I think about it often and I am deeply ashamed that it took me so long to get my mental health under control. One event in particular haunts me: your tenth birthday party, when I acted with physical violence toward our family dog in front of your friends. I still think about that day and how you must have felt.

I'll see you on the other side. Whether I mean that literally or figuratively will depend on the competency of Dr. Khayatian.

Love,
Dad

Your Sister Is Having an Emotional Experience in Target

Jules,
Just called u but it went to VM ...

That email u forwarded me from Dad is insane and at the same time I got a very similar letter ... hes talking about all these memories from when I was really little and like the nicknames he called me when I was a baby ... Like he said it looked like I had a receding hairline when I was born so he called me Salieri (???) after Mozarts enemy or something? Then he said to make sure Stuart keeps practicing the violin ...

Dude what if Dad knows he is about to die?! Maybe that's why he is sending us these emails like his life is already over. Obviously that would be a fucked up lie for him to tell since he told us not to come home for the surgery but maybe he was just trying to make it easier on us???? Should we go home now or is it already too late ...

Ugh now Im like hyperventilating and no one around me

is even noticing bc its fucking Arizona so im sure they all just think I am on meth . . .

I just climbed in one of the tents in the camping section and I am not coming out til you call me back. Bye world . . .

J

Your Dad, Who Just Got a New Lease on Life, Has Another New Lease on Life

Julie and Jane,

Thank you for the floral delivery. Unfortunately, as flowers are not allowed in the intensive care unit, they were discarded by an attending nurse. That said, she mentioned the arrangement was impressively robust.

You'll be pleased to know that in addition to surviving the procedure, I have emerged with a new appreciation for what is truly most important in life, a philosophy that combines my core values system with the Eastern influence of my beloved.

It's called filial piety. I'll give you both a moment to Google the term.

As you can see, all it means is an emphasis on respect and devotion toward one's elders and ancestors. Throughout Chinese history, the emperors invoked the concept often, wishing for their subjects to serve them with the loyalty and devotion they would show their own parents.

To that end, I'd like to request that you prioritize visits and calls home in the coming years and do your best to attend to my needs when you're a guest in my home. Don't hesitate to ask if you have any questions.

Love,
Dad

Your Sister, on Your Dad's New Lease on Life

OMG DAD'S EMAIL WTF . . . ???

K well . . . the good news is Dad lived . . .

But ughhhhhhh so much for him changing into a better person . . .

He cannot expect us to spend our lives waiting on him hand and foot! If he wants Stuart to bring him tea and serenade him with his little fucking violin he is welcome to do that on his own time!!!

Jane

Your Mom Is Really Connecting with Her Lawyer as a Woman

Dear Julie,

I just wanted to let you know that I took your advice about Dad and have hired a lawyer to negotiate with his lawyer about his request regarding my alimony payments. Hopefully this will relieve some of the pressure you've felt to "mediate" between us.

I also wanted to reassure you that I did a lot of research

in choosing who would be best to represent me, asking my usual "tribe" of friends from temple who they might recommend. Many women in the Temple Emanuel community have ex-husbands who are doctors and academics, so I figured they would know who has a lot of experience dealing with narcissists. When they all unanimously recommended Susan Distenfeld, I knew I would be in good hands!

What I didn't know is that Susan would also become one of my best friends. From the moment I walked into her office, the two of us just "clicked." We have so much in common—we both grew up in the Bronx with incredibly strong mother figures who worked in food service. We both attended women's colleges, where we both found ourselves having complicated feelings toward a female roommate but eventually decided that despite the strong emotional connection, we preferred men sexually.

Susan also shares my passion for talking to strangers. When we hit the town, watch out! Just yesterday at Whole Foods, we befriended a lovely cashier named Miguel who is trying to get his wife and young daughter up here from El Salvador. By the time we had checked out with our twelve items (he works in the express lane), Susan had taken on Miguel as a client and I had told him that his wife and daughter are welcome to move into my condo temporarily if they have any difficulty finding an apartment right away.

Another thing Susan and I have in common is our strong bonds with our grown children. I've told her all about you, and she would love to meet you whenever you next come home. If there are any art exhibits you'd like to see at the Museum of Fine Arts, that might be a nice place for us to go.

I've attached the museum calendar to this e-mail if you'd like to pick a weekend.

I guess I should "fess up." I have a hidden agenda: Susan has a son named Adam who works at the Museum of Fine Arts.

I know the last time I tried to fix you up you said you didn't think I understood what you found attractive, but I'm very confident that this time would be different. Adam is just adorable. Susan's ex-husband was African American, so he has beautiful caramel-colored skin but light eyes that are still very gentle and soulful, like two turquoise lagoons. Adam also sounds like a very interesting person. He works at the museum café, selling various kinds of salads.

Okay, honey, I should get going. I'm meeting Loni at Brookline Booksmith for a reading by a Bosnian poet who is in town teaching at Emerson. It's very important to me that Loni knows she's not being replaced by Susan. Of course, she hasn't explicitly said she feels that way, but I've noticed she never laughs at Susan's jokes, which are always hysterical.

Of course, this could also just be a case of "lost in translation." Susan's humor is very brash, in a style common among many Jewish women. Although Loni can be fun loving in her own way, at the end of the day she's still a Protestant woman from Indiana.

Let me know which of these museum events interest you.

Love,
Mom

PS—Did you see Elizabeth Warren's interview on LATE NIGHT WITH RACHEL MADDOW?

Your Dad Figured He Would
Keep Putting You in the Middle

Julie,

I enjoyed your latest article on "Hollywood Hotties with Receding Hairlines."

Also, I finally heard back from your mother about our financial negotiations, though I was required to enlist legal counsel to get a response out of her. It turns out she has also enlisted the services of a lawyer, Susan Distenfeld.

You've got to be kidding me. Check out this woman's ratings on Yelp: one star out of five. Her office appears to be located above a Quiznos—and as a comedy writer, you will appreciate her reviews.

I can only imagine what would happen if doctors were allowed to practice medicine with the same impairments your mother's lawyer seems to have—you'd have a lot of patients showing up to the hospital with a sprained ankle and walking out with full-blown AIDS.

It's been a while since you've called me to chat. Any particular reason?

Dad

Your Mom's New Best Friend Sucks

Dear Julie and Jane,

I wanted to let you girls know that I went through a trauma this week. I'm all right now and I don't want you to worry, but I did want to send you this e-mail so I can help prevent

SUSANNA FOGEL

the same thing that happened to me from happening to either of you.

As you know, I've been getting very close to Susan, the lawyer who has been helping me handle my alimony case with your dad. As I said, we have so much in common: we're both very involved in our congregations, we share many of the same philosophies about parenting, we have both seen every episode of *Law & Order: SVU*. And I think I told you girls we went to a couple of tango classes in Somerville together.

So you can imagine how hurtful it was when I opened my mail earlier this week and found a bill from Susan charging me for every hour we had spent together.

Of course, I would expect her to charge me for the time we spent in her office discussing the legal case itself. But Susan had also charged me for the tango class, the ninety minutes we spent at Panera Bread having lunch after one of those meetings (where we talked mostly about what it was like for her to grow up in a military family), and the two hours when we went to Coolidge Corner Theatre to see the new movie with Colin Firth, during which we didn't talk at all. If I had known that movie ticket would cost me $350, I would have gone to see it alone. I've already seen it three times.

Julie, I don't know if you contacted Susan's son Adam yet to try to meet up with him. If you have and you feel he's someone you could fall in love with, I hope what I've just said won't make you have second thoughts. The most important thing to me is that you girls are happy. But if you haven't reached out to Adam, I wanted you to know about this because in my experience as a psychoanalyst, parents' values (or lack thereof!) always affect the way their children interact with others, even subconsciously.

And for both of you girls, I just wanted to tell you what happened so you can make sure to be careful about who you decide to let into your life. Of course, part of being an adult is getting to make new and exciting connections with people from very different backgrounds and upbringings, but as you're getting to know someone, just make sure there is no "fine print."

If you don't feel comfortable asking this up front, one thing you could do is just ask someone what they do for a living right away. That way at least you can decide how risky it is to spend time with them and if that's a risk you're willing to take.

Luckily, there are plenty of people who are no risk at all. Just yesterday I met a new friend at the Zumba class at Healthworks. Her name is Divya and she was raised in Pakistan, where she was a nationally ranked badminton player! Obviously an athlete is not someone who could consider our time together a business transaction, so I asked her if she'd like to come with me to the Louisa May Alcott museum for their annual exhibit of the various teas and biscuits that were popular in that time period. We had a great time, and I can "rest easy" knowing that I'm not going to get an invoice in the mail! On the other hand, someone who is a lawyer, social worker, or mystic could try to do what Susan did. I think it will take longer for me to trust someone like that in the future.

Of course I understand that as a psychoanalyst, I'm someone people may have avoided in the past for that reason. It's something I never thought about before, but it certainly explains some of my interactions with people over the years!

One more thing. When I told Divya what happened with Susan, she recommended I give her a negative review on "Yelp." Have either of you girls heard of "Yelp"? I'm not sure if it's a website or new software I have to get for my computer, but I would love to figure it out so I can do what she suggested and try to heal my trauma that way. If one of you has time tomorrow and can give me a call and walk me through "Yelp," I'd really appreciate it!

I just charged up my laptop, so I won't even need to have it plugged in while we talk.

With constellations of love,
Mom

Your Sister, on Your Mom Getting Fucked With

OMG MOMS EMAIL . . .

I feel so bad for her. Ppl should not be takin advantage of her like that! Like she's so smart but she can be so innocent sometimes u know?

So do u wanna be the one to teach her how to use Yelp? Sorry but I don't have 7 hours free tomorrow bahahahaha

Your Mom
Wanted to Run Her First Yelp Review by You

Hi Jules,

I got your message about having plans all day today and not being able to teach me "Yelp.com." I guess Jane has plans all day too.

Luckily, it turns out my condo actually has an in-house website tutor ... Loni! She was very happy to help me. Loni is a whiz with computers. We were joking that she should charge people in the building for her services and we came up with some hilarious names she could have for her company. I've forgotten what the specific names are now, but many of them made reference to the fact that Loni just dyed her hair a really striking shade of red.

Anyway, after my "lesson," Loni had to get going to pick up her daughter Carolyn at the airport (Carolyn and her husband don't land until 7:55, but the traffic between here and Logan has been just horrific lately due to construction in the Ted Williams Tunnel, so we figured it was better for her to be early than late). So she didn't have time to stay while I wrote the review itself, but I told her I could handle that part on my own. I took several writing classes in fiction, nonfiction, and journalism in college and have always gotten the feedback that my writing is extremely persuasive.

Still, I'm lucky enough to have a professional writer for a daughter! I wondered if you wouldn't mind taking a quick look at this. I know you said you were busy today, but this should just take a minute. If you're out, don't worry about

it—you can take a look when you get home. No rush—
again, I know how busy you are.

I'll just sit here with my finger on the "Send" button until
I hear from you!

Love,
Mom

(SEE BELOW FOR THE YELP REVIEW)

To: Susandistenfeld@distenfeldandassociates.com
c/o Yelp.com
Dear Susan,
This is Barbara Feller. As you know, I am a former client
who also considered you to be a friend. Then I discovered
that you engaged me in our friendship under false pretenses
and considered all our time together to be "on the clock."
When I first found this out, I thought about hiring a second
lawyer to sue you for malpractice, then decided to take the
"high road" instead rather than stoop to your level. That is
something I have always made an effort to do in my personal relationships, as a psychoanalyst.

My analytic training also makes me confident that whatever caused you to behave so unethically must be very
painful for you and rooted in some trauma of your own. I
urge you to get professional help so you can work through
that pain and not inflict those childhood wounds on any
more innocent women.

Technically, you already have been seeing a therapist. If
I took a page out of your book, I could bill you for all the
hours we spent together during which I listened and gave
you advice about your son's reliance on marijuana, your

mother's obesity, and your conflicting feelings about moving to Newton Highlands. But I feel that charging you would be a conflict of interest. I wish you had felt that way as well.

In the future, if people ask me to recommend a divorce lawyer, I will not recommend you. As you can see, I have given you one star.

Sincerely,
Barbarafeller1948@aol.com

Your Dad Does Not Approve of Your Choice of Birthday Gift

Julie,

As a first order of business, your voice-mail mailbox is full.

I wanted to let you know we received the Solar Robot you sent Stuart for his birthday. Although he appreciated the gesture, Stuart noticed a warning label on the back of the box alerting us to the fact that traces of lead may be found in the product. I contacted Amazon's Customer Service department and expect they will give me a credit, with which I intend to help my son find a less carcinogenic way to celebrate turning eight.

I don't think any permanent damage was done to your relationship with your little brother, as I explained to Stuart that you were not purposely trying to kill him. That said, I think a personal note of apology from you would go a long way. I am very proud to report that he is now e-mailing at a fifth-grade level.

Dad

Your Hot Cousin Paul,
with Whom You Always Had a Vibe,
Heard about Your Autobiographical Novel

Hey Julie—

What's up? My mom said she had lunch with you the other day while you were visiting an old friend from college who just got diagnosed with breast cancer. Sorry to hear that.

Anyway, my mom also mentioned you're working on a book about a family, loosely based on ours. How loosely are you thinking? Is everyone from our actual family a character in it? I'm just curious how closely you will be basing it on our real family members and the relationships you have with each of them, and if you're going to include a lot of details that would make it obvious who everyone is based on.

Just asking because I'm sure that your interpretation of some relationships you have with some of your family members is skewed, and I wouldn't want you to be in a situation where you're accusing anyone of anything that might have happened when people were much younger or drunk or whatever. I just don't think adding anything that could get them in trouble with their spouses and jeopardize the happiness and stability of their new families would end up being worth it.

Anyway, you get what I'm saying.

See you on the Cape for my dad's seventieth.

Paul

Your Dad, Who Got Married at Twenty-Two, Has Some Wisdom about Navigating the Singles Scene

Dear Julie,

I took Stuart to see Dr. Leung today. She said she's never seen straighter, or whiter, teeth in a child his age. She also told me that according to your mother, you've been having some trouble meeting Mr. Right out there in Los Angeles.

When Mei-Ling and I met, we immediately knew we were meant to be, and neither of us has had any doubts, insecurities, or concerns about our relationship since. Just make sure to hold whomever you meet to that standard.

I hope this helps you move forward.

Love,
Dad

Your Grandma Would Love to Get You Laid

Julie, Your mom sent me the article you wrote for the internet about Prince William. I agree with you that the fox hunting outfit was not his Best Summer Look. Now let me ask you a Q. My Scrabble buddy, Rena, has a grandson who just moved to LA. He's starting some sort of business there. Anyway, he's unattached. I saw his picture, and he's pretty sexy. Rena said he's very nice, so he might be boring, but you may as well get a free dinner out of it. Can we hook it up? You met Rena. She's the one who's always talking about the Holocaust.

The Nice Jewish Guy
Your Grandma Is Setting You Up With
Is a Little Self-Conscious

Hey Julie,

My name is Isaac Halpern-Miller and I got your e-mail from my grandmother, who is neighbors with your grandmother at North Park Village back in MA. Hopefully she warned you that I might be dropping you a line—if not, I bet you've already sent this e-mail to spam, or reported me to Google for hacking, or are calling your bank to cancel all your credit cards because you think I'm a Nigerian scam artist . . . or all of the above.

But if you're even still reading this far in—and again, I totally understand if you're not—let me know if you feel like grabbing a drink sometime. My hours are pretty flexible since I'm self-employed. (I run a startup with two buddies from B-school; more on that if we meet up, if you haven't already run screaming from this e-mail and then smashed your laptop with a hammer and thrown all the pieces into the LA River . . .)

IHM

PS—You can be honest if you think this is too weird!

The Nice Jewish Guy You Drunkenly Slept With Had a Great Time Last Night

Hey there,

I just got home from work to find my condo empty, which can only mean one thing: you were abducted by aliens who now have you in custody on the planet Zog, where they erased all your memories and are training you to be a lean, mean killing machine in their army.

No, but seriously, I take it you found your way home. I'm glad I was there to take care of you last night, even if it was all my fault we drank so much. I really shouldn't have brought up our grandmas and how much it's going to suck when they die.

But hey, it all worked out, right? Just FYI, I'm not an asshole player or anything—I definitely want to take you out again. I was thinking, one of our investors owns this B&B in wine country. Pick a weekend in May.

Isaac

PS—I just remembered that joke you made about the bartender's mustache and laughed again.

The Nice Jewish Guy You Casually Slept With Just Wanted to Check In

Hey there Julie!

What's up? It's Isaac (from last Friday). Just wanted to drop you a line and make sure you got my e-mail the other day—sometimes the e-mail server at my office is a little glitchy and my e-mails don't go through. Anyway, if you did get my e-mail and just haven't had a chance to reply, that's totally cool! Take your time. But if you didn't get an e-mail from me, let me know and I will resend ASAP. Or, third option, if you did get it and already replied to me and I'm the one who didn't get it, then so sorry, but would you mind resending?

This has been happening with a lot of my e-mails. Not just yours.

Talk soon!

I

Sent from a Tiny Robot Monitored by the US Government

The Nice Jewish Guy You Blew Off Would Like to Defend Himself

Julie,

Don't worry. I'm not writing to ask you for anything. Reading this e-mail will only take five seconds of your precious time. But maybe that's still too much of a burden for you, since that's more than you were able to spare from your busy day to do me the courtesy of replying to either of my other e-mails? Or maybe you got a new e-mail address in the last week and just forgot to tell me! Or things "got really crazy" this week and you didn't have time to write back? You're gonna have to do a lot better than that, because at this point in my life, I've heard everything. Not that you're even planning on replying to this letter either—why break your pattern?! Whatever. I thought you were different because we had a good time the other night and you seemed pretty smart, but I guess you're just another girl who's looking for some guy who drives a Tesla and knows all the right people so you can get ahead in your Hollywood career. You go, girl! It's all about who you know! Glad to see none of the clichés about women in LA being shallow and status obsessed are true! Oh, wait, they all are!

Not that you even care about my side of this, or anything else that doesn't directly benefit your life, but just for the record, I thought we should just be friends anyway. If you had bothered to reply to me and let me finish what I was going to say, you would have known that. I invited a bunch of people on that trip to wine country. But don't worry—I don't even want that anymore. I really don't need any more one-sided friendships in my life.

Oh, also, I didn't mention this before, but my grandma said your grandma's a bitch.

Bye!

Isaac

Your Grandma Rose Heard What Happened with the Nice Jewish Guy

Julie, I saw Rena today. She told me what happened with you and her grandson. Sounds like you dodged a bullet. If a grown man tells his grandma everything he does in the sack, he has some funny ideas about what it means to be a man. He sounds like a kid named Philipp who was my first kiss back in Seattle. Then he went off to fight in World War Two. He was killed on his first day, just climbing out of the plane.

Your Intrauterine Device Has Some Thoughts on Your Love Life

Hey lady,

What's up? I hope it's okay that I'm reaching out to/from you like this. I know you've been saying in therapy that you want to improve your communication with those closest to you. At least I think that's what you said: I can only hear your sessions clearly on the days you wear skirts. (What does Dr. Fleming look like, btw? I just keep picturing Lorraine Bracco.) Anyway, obviously you and I have a pretty intimate relationship since you literally trust me with your life (slash the prevention of new ones, haha) on a daily basis. Or, let's be honest, not daily—every two months-ish. More since your last birthday. That's kind of what I wanted to talk to you about.

Sooooo, real talk: maybe it's just the view from where I'm sitting (#yourlowercervix) but it seems like ever since you turned thirty-two, you've lowered your standards for sexual partners. Granted, I only know part of the story since I only see the one part of them, but I think it's safe to say I know you better than you know yourself. And I like to think I'm pretty observant about the outside world in general, even though I'm internal by nature. My point is I can tell you're selling yourself short.

Like that guy, Marc, you met on Tinder who said you were his first Tinder date, and then he suddenly took himself off Tinder after your second date, but you didn't feel like you could ask him about it on your third date because it was too early, but then he disappeared for two weeks anyway and when he finally resurfaced he claimed he'd been in Buenos Aires and forgot his phone charger, or they didn't have the right converters for American chargers there, or something.

Seriously?

I could not have agreed more with the eight friends you called for advice that you should not get drinks with him again. But you did, and by extension, so did I. And what happened later that night can only be described as a violation of both of our dignities. Not to be all "I told you so," but I knew neither of us was ever gonna see him again.

Or that bike messenger you met at the Cha Cha Lounge the night before your birthday. I don't think I caught his name, but I definitely heard him use the word "sarcastical" and discuss with pride how much money he saved the year he lived in a storage unit and took all his showers at the gym. I know you were really drunk that night and thirty-two is a weird age to be turning—I remember you talking to Dr. Fleming about that—but still. You have so much going for you. And you're probably beautiful—at least, you are on the inside.

And . . . okay, I wasn't going to bring this up, but can we talk about what happened with your ex-boyfriend from New York? Granted, I never met Ben when you guys were dating since you just used condoms back then, but he seems like such a nice guy, and obviously he's still totally in love with you. I know Amy's wedding weekend was really emotional, and I heard you telling your friends it made you think about Raj, but that's all the more reason why sleeping with Ben, knowing he was just gonna get super invested in you again, was kind of cruel—to him and to me. 'Cause not to be a martyr here, but it was like his entire life force was trying to put a baby in you. Both times. I was like a goalkeeper at the fucking World Cup for you that night. And then I woke up feeling sad for all three of us.

Anyway, you get the point I'm making here. I really hope this doesn't seem like an attack. I know I have a reputation for being cold and sterile, and a lot of people have said it really hurts to let me in. Just ask the multiple hate blogs on the internet about it. (Related: would you mind asking Dr. Fleming for advice on how I can stop going into WebMD/ Yahoo Answers click holes when I can't sleep? Would love her thoughts.) But trust me, this is all coming from a place of love. It's not about me at all, because let's be honest: when you meet The One, you won't need me anymore. They'll bury me in that hazardous waste bin in the exam room where we first met, next to something slimy, and I'll never get to meet your baby. But it will all be worth it to me, because that's the kind of friend I am.

Let me know if you wanna talk further. I'm always here for/in you.

Big heart,
Mirena™

Your Dad's Friend
Who Makes You a Little Uncomfortable
Is Happy to Help

Dear Julie,

I'm sorry it's taken me a couple of hours to respond to your e-mail. I spent the afternoon competing in the final round of a tennis tournament here on Nantucket. It was a fun day of being on my toes—turns out I was the only person who qualified who wasn't nationally ranked. A lot of sports pros have homes on the island.

Anyway, I'm so glad you reached out. I'd be more than happy to help you figure out what's happening with the mole on your back and whether it could be cancerous. And don't worry; I won't tell your dad you don't have health insurance. I'm very good at keeping secrets. Also, I was young once (not too long ago) and remember what it's like not to want to deprive yourself of the basic pleasures of youth in the name of being "responsible." I remember in medical school, I spent an entire semester crashing on a friend's couch so I could save my rent money and buy a motorcycle I'd had my eye on.

I think I've mentioned I ride motorcycles.

So let's talk about your skin. First, the basics: when did you first notice the mole, and has it changed shape or size since then? If not, you're probably in the clear, but just to make sure, why don't you send pix? Amateur (iPhone) photos are fine. Either way, even without seeing it, I'd probably advise you to have it removed. I know that's a little hard to do when you can't afford to pay a doctor in cash . . .

SUSANNA FOGEL

but I have it on good authority that some doctors will accept payment in the form of margaritas and road trips up the famous Pacific Coast Highway.

That's right; I'll be in California next weekend.

As it happens, I've been trying to schedule a trip out there to meet an old friend from Doctors Without Borders (Bosnia, late nineties, treating burn victims in Sarajevo). Howie actually lives up in Berkeley, but I figured why not fly into LAX on Friday, rent a car, head over to your apartment and we can do a little guerrilla surgery on that mole. (I'll bring all the tools; as long as you have a working gas stove, we're good to go. Believe me, I had less to work with in Bosnia.) After that, your prescription for a speedy recovery is to get the hell out of Dodge. I'll plan to get you a plane ticket back to LA from San Francisco for Sunday night, so you can be back in time for work on Monday. And of course, all meals, gas, and snacks along the way are on me. I'll also supply ample Joni Mitchell and Leonard Cohen.

Screw Obamacare—I think you'll find Larrycare much more effective. I've already put plane tickets on hold; just let me know if I can confirm.

Fondly,
Larry Shepherd

Your Mother's Goddaughter,
Who Makes High Six Figures,
Would Love to be Reimbursed

Dearest friends and family,

Thank you for journeying to the wilds of rural Canada to celebrate our special day with us! It was a weekend we'll never forget. It was especially meaningful for Kevin to see the three hundred people who mean the most to him take two flights, a ferry, and a half-day pedicab ride to gather on an undeveloped island he visited once as a kid.

Seriously, we cannot stop smiling.

Also, thanks to everyone who contributed to our Honeyfund. With your help, we'll be able to enjoy three weeks in St. Maarten without having to worry about anything, including hidden costs like snacks and magazines at the airport (thanks, Aunt Laura!), gas in the rental car (Uncle Frank, you're the best!), or the fee for renewing Kevin's passport (love you, Jane!).

In the meantime, as we get ready to leave on Saturday at 2:55 (sorry, did we mention we're excited about our trip?) we're scrambling to dot our Is and cross our Ts to close out with the vendors and venue. As you know, we stocked your cabins with food and wine, since there are no cars on the island and the one restaurant within walking distance is only open every other Wednesday. According to our calculations, the total amount we spent on food for each cabin was $120.35. If you wouldn't mind touching base with whomever you shared your cabin with to figure out how you want to divvy that up based on who ate what, that would be a huge help. A spreadsheet of everyone's contact information is attached, and a link to our PayPal is below!

Tot ziens! (That means "see you soon" in Dutch ☺)

Rachel and Kevin

Your Sister Has Some Thoughts on Your Mother's Goddaughter's Invoice

OMG DUDE RACHEL'S EMAIL IM DYING

. . . i am speechless . . . are u gonna send her money?? like why are you so fuckin cheap? sorry lady it was yr decision to have a wedding with everyone u have ever met! and whatever u can afford it isn't your husband a lawyer for red bull?

at the very least let yr guests know u are going to do this in advance. i wouldve just brought tigers milk bars from home—did i tell u tyler hooked up this crazy deal with this dude he lifts with at his gym who works at GNC? or fuck energy bars i couldve just brought tyler's gun and gone out into the wilderness and rustled us up some fuckin steaks! probs wouldnt have been smart to take a concealed weapon on the plane tho haha.

i dare u to send Rachel a check for like 30 cents and be like oh yes I ate an egg sandwich but then i got the shits so i didn't really digest it so yeah im just paying for half of it here you go byeeeeeeeee

jane

Ps—did dad send you his weird slideshow? like ok dude we know your wife got u editing software for yr computer calm down. also whyyyyyy did he pick a fuckin EMINEM song to go with the photos?! eminem is way past his prime just like you are old man! and that picture of his son in that plaid suit from the wedding?! I love how when u asked about it he was all STUART PICKED IT OUT HIMSELF. yikes that kid is gonna be so fucked in junior high . . .

Your Mom Has Some New Judgments She'd Like to Share

Hi sweetheart,

I just wanted to touch base and thank you and Jane for the beautiful "French Country" tablecloth you got me for my birthday! I put it on the big table in the dining room and have been eating dinner in there every night so I can look at it. It matches perfectly with the Russian doll salt and pepper shakers. Of course, since I eat most of my meals alone, one of the sides of the tablecloth is getting a lot more "wear and tear" than the other, but that's okay! I don't mind eating alone. I'm not worried about choking.

I also wanted to keep you posted on something that happened with Rabbi Josh last week. I don't want you to feel awkward if you are working together on his television show, but because you didn't mention anything about that at my bat mitzvah and you seemed to be avoiding him at the reception, I assume you haven't had a chance to respond to his e-mail yet. I wanted to say don't feel like you have to help him on my account—not after what happened last week.

I think I mentioned during your visit home that Loni

and I thought it would be fun to spend Easter and Passover together and introduce each other to our respective faiths.

First, I joined Loni for Easter services at her church. (Do they call them services? I would look it up now, but I'm not sure how to do that without losing this e-mail!) The atmosphere was very inclusive, and I enjoyed the festive meal we ate after. Why don't Jews eat more goose?

Anyway, then I took her to Temple Emanuel so she could see the famous Rabbi Josh "in action." (Of course, she had met him at my bat mitzvah, but I did most of the performing that day!)

Unfortunately, we both got a window into a darker side of Rabbi Josh. Usually he finds a way to work some current events into the sermon when he talks about ethics and community, and this time, he chose to talk about the politics of the West Bank. I've always thought of Rabbi Josh as a very fair person, so I was surprised when he spoke of how Israel has a divine right to the land, in a manner I found to be very extreme. Loni thought so too—during secretarial school, she shared an office with a woman named Amira who was Palestinian, and they became very close, so she obviously thinks the whole situation is far more complicated. And so do I—I recently saw a foreign film at Coolidge Corner that showed a group of Palestinian children growing up in the shadow of war, in which many were harassed and tormented by the occupying Israeli army. The movie was fictional, but it was based on a true story.

After he finished, I went up to Rabbi Josh and asked why he doesn't support a two-state solution. He became very defensive and implied that I was disloyal to my religion for even suggesting it, which was incredibly insulting. I left before the wine and challah sing-along. That's how angry I was.

Loni was very good-natured about the whole thing. She took me to a nearby bar (the one where you always meet your friends from high school when you come home) and we shared a pitcher of sangria—your favorite! After a couple of glasses, she showed me how to log into Rabbi Josh's Facebook account so we could look at some pictures of him. In most of them, it looks like he's trying to pose to be a model or something. And he included some photographs of his wife that were very provocative—almost like he was trying to show her off. I think he might be an egomaniac. I decided not to renew my membership at the temple—at least, not as long as he's presiding over things like a sinister Pied Piper!

How is your new apartment? Did you get the 20% off coupon to Bed Bath and Beyond I sent you?

Love,
Mom

Your Chinese Stepmother Wishes to Honor Your Day Job

Dear Julie,
It's your stepmom, having written to let you know that I deeply admired your recent online article about celebrities who pretend to come from other eras entirely. This topic was of special interest to me, as my culture has great

reverence for bygone dynasties and does not tolerate acts of historical impersonation.

Particularly offensive was one actress you discussed. About her work, I was previously unfamiliar. Since acquainting myself with her, I have imposed censorship on exposing myself to all future works involving this celebrity and her mockery of time itself.

Thank you sincerely for cautioning me against the art of Zooey Deschanel.

Yours truly,
Mei-Ling Feller

Your Dad, Who Just Joined Facebook, Has Another Request

Julie,
Thank you for accepting my friendship.

I have some good news. I have decided to compile my haikus into a book and self-publish it. Mei-Ling provided the illustrations, as she studied fine art back in Shanghai. A link to the manuscript is attached.

I would appreciate it if you could post on your Facebook page about my book of haikus. That way, everyone in your community will find out about it.

Dad

Your Mom,
Who Had Six Glasses of Wine Tonight,
Was Just Thinking about You

Hola honey!!!!!!!!!!!!!!!

I wish I could write upside-down exclamation points like they do here in Spain but I am typing this on my computer which is American and I don't think they make that key on American computers. I wonder if I can find an Apple Store here in Barcelona where I can rent a new keyboard when in Rome. Not literally Rome because obviously I am not in Italy, but Rome in the sense of the old adage, "When in Rome, do as the Romans do," meaning use the upside-down exclamation point!

I want to be honest, honey: I am stoned.

I also had two bottles of wine tonight with Loni after a wonderful meal of paella eaten on Las Ramblas. That's the main drag here. The manager of our hotel, Felipe, recommended a terrific restaurant called Dos Palomas with a window overlooking a very large and colorful Gaudí. I think I told you about Felipe in my last e-mail. He's the one who has an adolescent son who competes in something called a "rap battle" and will be coming to Los Angeles for a contest in May—I hope it's okay that I gave Felipe your number for his son. The waiter at Dos Palomas was a very tall man who looked like he might be part North African— around here there are so many beautiful people of mixed ethnicity. He let us have our own little "wine tasting" so we could choose the bottle we liked best. Loni and I couldn't decide between red and white so we had both. We stayed for hours just talking and laughing until the end of the night, when the waiter's friend came to the bar to play cards and brought with him a bag of something. I can't remember the name in Spanish right now but the gist is that it was hashish and Loni and I figured why not.

Being here reminds me of the last time I was in Spain, one summer during graduate school. I haven't really told you about this part of my life, so I hope it's okay that I'm sharing it now. I briefly had a Spanish boyfriend named Federico who was studying politics; we met while studying for finals in a Syrian café a few blocks from Columbia that served wonderful Middle Eastern sandwiches. I was drawn to Federico because he was different. At that time, all the other men on campus were only passionate about one thing (protesting the Vietnam War) but Federico wanted to escape it all and move back to Spain. He invited me to spend the summer with his family on an olive farm, and as you can imagine that seemed very romantic, so I accepted. But it turned out to be a fantasy. For one thing, Federico was culturally very macho. His parents were very nice and welcomed me into their home, but it became clear they wanted their son to have a traditional wife to cook and clean, and I was studying to have my own career as an analyst. I knew that sort of traditional life wasn't for me, so I told Federico I had to leave. He became hysterical. At one point he even threw a plate across the room and I thought, I have to get out of here. I walked five miles to the train station. Unfortunately, I had given up my apartment in New York for the summer, so I decided to stay in Europe for another month. I took a train all the way to Amsterdam and found a spare room for rent in the home of a very artistic couple.

Jens and Mieke and I cooked meals together, and they showed me their work every night. I even posed for some of Jens's paintings that were very impressionistic and haunting, like the work of Hieronymus Bosch. In one of them, my face becomes a clown's face, and the ground underneath me is made of lava and is rising up to swallow the earth. There was something very sexual about Jens's work, and in fact, one night Jens and Mieke asked me to join them in some sexual experimentation. At that time in my life, I had only slept with two people—my first boyfriend, Simon, who became a mathematician, and Federico—so I was curious to try it. The touching felt good and very intimate. Mieke had grown up on a horse farm where her parents raised Hanoverians, and she was a skilled horsewoman, that much was clear. But I could tell Jens had feelings for me that were more than just physical, so I came back to the States. The night I got back to New York, I went to a jazz club to meet my friend Polly, and that's when I met your dad. Did you know your dad used to love jazz? Even during the busiest time of medical school and his residency, he would make the time to hear music and go to museums. Your dad had lots of passions then, before his depression got so much worse. I wish you had had a chance to meet that version of him.

It's funny that I just called him "your" dad. Remember when we were still married and I used to just call him "Dad"?

Okay, sweetie, I should head to sleep. But first I'm going to eat the rest of this danish we bought at a stand from a

SUSANNA FOGEL

wonderful young woman named Margarita. Loni and I have visited her every day since we got here. Margarita has very curly hair and reminds me of you. Have you ever thought about how there are people just like you and me all over the world who look and act so similar to us, but they aren't us? I wish I could send you a piece of this danish so you could taste how delicious it is.

Love,
Mom

Your Mother's Goddaughter Just Has a Couple Super-Quick Things Before You Meet Her Baby

Dear Friends!
Rachel and Kevin here. We have some news. For those of you who celebrated our wedding with us two years ago, remember the part where we both said we had found the love of our lives in each other? Well, we don't know how to tell you this, but it turns out we were wrong. Because we've both met someone else . . .

Our first child, Aurelia Spruce Mavis Kivowitz-Finch! Aurelia Spruce was born weighing eight pounds, four ounces in Room 421 of New York Methodist Hospital between 1:29:55 and 1:32:13pm (from crowning to final toe) with four hairs on her head and a slightly discolored placenta due to tiny flecks of fecal matter in the womb. A time-lapse video diary is attached so you can witness all this in more detail.

Now that she's home from the hospital, Aurelia Spruce is super excited to meet you! But first, as much as we hate to be "those parents" (we're gagging even writing this), we'd love it if you could take a second to glance over this short list of dos and don'ts before you schedule a visit. For our friends who are already parents, this stuff is all probably second nature. For our friends who aren't, don't worry. It'll happen for you.

—Immunizations: We'd love it if you were all up to date on your basic boosters (whooping cough, measles, mumps, and rubella). While you're at it, it would also be great if you could swing by CVS or Rite Aid and get the newly patented black plague vaccination, Bubonicil. Unfortunately, since Bubonicil is still in Phase 1 clinical trials and not yet approved by the FDA, it's not covered under normal health insurance. Luckily, it's relatively reasonably priced at a cost of $750 to $800 per shot in a series of four shots, administered anally.

—Other tests: To all the single ladies (and gents!), we're super jealous of all the fun you're having! We'd just love it if you could also grab a quick HIV test before you come by. Again, once you become parents, you'll understand why we're taking these kinds of precautions (of course, if your results come back positive, that may end up being a nonissue). No need to mail us the test results or anything—we trust you! Scan/e-mail is totally fine.

—For our friends who live in prewar buildings: Congratulations on your elegant, timeless home and its place in

New York's history! It would just be great if you could have your house inspected by a state-certified agency to ensure that no coat of paint manufactured before 1978 remains on the walls. If it does, please take a moment to repaint your home and dry clean your clothing to remove any traces of lead dust.

—Talking: Once you're here, it would be great if you could use correct grammar and syntax around Aurelia Spruce. Not a huge deal; this is just a fancy way of saying please avoid any abbreviations, regional accents, or colloquialisms until she becomes linguistic. Obviously this doesn't apply to our London-based friends, who are encouraged to exaggerate their pronunciation and mannered idiosyncrasies while interacting with our little one.

—Gifts: Gifts are not necessary! Your presence as a guest in our home is gift enough. However, if you do choose to bring a gift for Aurelia Spruce, thank you! We also thank you in advance for shopping within a gender-neutral color palette. If you've been keeping up with recent studies, you may have heard that prolonged exposure to the color pink has been linked to insecurity, a high risk for passive-aggressive behavior, and a diminished likelihood of a leadership position in the entertainment industry. The color blue, meanwhile, is associated with deficient empathy, an adult-onset tendency to respond monosyllabically during arguments with romantic partners, and a lack of awareness about the extent to which male privilege facilitates accomplishment in the workplace. Scary stuff!

—Polka dots: Aurelia Spruce is terrified of polka dots. It would be great if you could avoid wearing any polka dots while visiting our home. This includes socks. Please also take a second to check your clothing for stains, as a stain often resembles a polka dot.

That's it! We know how busy you guys are (that's the thing about having rock stars for friends!) so if you don't have time to do the above, don't sweat it; you can have virtual hang time with our girl. To add her on Skype, just search her name ("AureliaSpruceMavis"). She's the second one who comes up in Brooklyn.

Much love,
Team Kivowitz-Finch
(Rachel, Kevin, Aurelia Spruce, and Dachsund
Faustus)

Your Grandma Rose Has Some News about Her Nemesis

Julie, Give me a call sometime. I could use some cheering up. Maureen died. No one here liked her, but it reminded us our days are numbered.

What happened is a mystery. The fellow with the tattoos from the front desk went to her room to fix her dishwasher and found her dead on the couch. She was in the middle of watching that movie about all the bridesmaids. Maybe she died laughing.

SUSANNA FOGEL

Your Sister Would Like to Discuss
Your Dad's Facebook Page

uhhhhhh did you notice dads outfit in his new FB photo? im not even talking about the part where hes wearing timberlands with an orange fly fishing hat (????) but um look at his shorts cause i think you can kinda see part of his junk hanging out the left side?????!!!!! am i hallucinating???? omg i cant even type right now im laughin so hard but seriously WTF do we do about this situation? i mean the man has a right to know hes puttin his shit on blast but THAT CONVERSATION IS SO AWKWARD. Also um am I a pervert for even noticing dad's dick lol

    ugh I miss u and wanna tell u about this guy i might be in love with so call me when u can . . . he may or may not be my landlord cuz i'm a fuckin idiot haha.

xx Jane

Your Uncle Figured a Mass E-mail
Was the Easiest Way to Discuss His Sexuality

Greetings, Family Feller!!
I'm not sure where to start, so I figured I'd do as I usually do and let science do the talking. Most of you know Newton's Third Law of Motion—for every action, there is an equal and opposite reaction. I've always found it to be true about life in general. Every time something bad happens, something good is just around the corner.

First comes the bad news: I won't be making it back to Boston for Thanksgiving this year. Ron, my roommate, has been having some trouble with his blood pressure lately, and he collapsed at a dress rehearsal with his students on Sunday night and ended up in the ER. I've decided to stay in Denver and have dinner at the hospital with him on Thursday. Talk about a turkey of a day!

But as Newton's Law would have it, something equally exciting happened . . .

Ron proposed to me last night. We've actually been a couple since 2009.

Whew. That felt good to just come out (so to speak!) and say! I'll start at the beginning: I'm sure you all remember when Ron first moved into the spare bedroom of my condo and I introduced him as a new friend I'd met at a teachers' conference who was going through a divorce and getting back on his feet. All of that was technically true, but I fudged some of those details. When we met at the conference, Ron was still married to his ex-wife, but the reason they got divorced is that we fell in love there. I can't explain it except to say we both felt like the other person woke us up, even though we didn't even realize we had been sleeping our whole lives. As you know, I'd spent most of my life being pretty overweight, and I always blamed that for why I felt so strange around women when people would try to set me up on dates. No matter how nice a gal it was, I felt like I was standing outside my own body watching myself. I was always stuck in my own head, wondering why my heart wasn't feeling anything. With Ron, I suddenly stopped thinking. My body and my mind became one and I just knew what to do. Ron felt the same way. That's when we both realized we were gay, and Ron decided to leave his wife back in Salt Lake.

Of course, I wanted to call all of you right away, but Ron asked me to wait to tell anyone until he could tell his parents, because that was a funky situation. Ron comes from a pretty traditional Mormon family, and as I'm sure you know, in that religion, being gay is a real no-no. His parents didn't even approve of him being a drama teacher, and they kept telling him to work on his marriage to Jeanette and try to patch that up. It just never seemed like the right time, and before we knew it, years were going by and no one knew the truth. But now, enough is enough. If Ron's health scare has taught us anything, it's that life is too short not to be honest about who you are and who you love. We decided to call that "Ron and Ken's First Law of Emotion!"

Have a great Thanksgiving. I'll miss all of you and our holiday traditions, especially the "food coma walk" Julie and Jane and I always take to CVS after dinner to get our ceremonial bottle of Pepto-Bismol! Hopefully next year, Ron will come back east with me and we can show him how it's done. Julie and Jane, he knows you girls have always been like the daughters I never had, and I hope you'll start to see Ron as another uncle now too . . . not just the guy who's crashing in my extra bedroom! (Another detail we fudged—that's not where he sleeps.)

For whoever takes over for me on pumpkin-pie duty, my secret is I whip the egg whites before I add them to the batter. Ron taught me that. Hey, Mom, you always told me to find a wife who can cook!

Love,
Ken

PS—I'll try to give you a ring Friday when you're all together and tell you about the proposal! It was really romantic. Ron had one of his male nurses (who has to be James Franco's long-lost twin!) page me over the PA at the hospital to ask for my hand in marriage. Ron actually had him use the phrase "hand in marriage"! He has such a flair for drama. No wonder his students win at the Shakespeare & Company Monologuefest every year!

Your Sister Just Got Your Uncle's E-mail about His Sexuality

OMG THIS EXPLAINS EVERYTHINGGGGGGGGG
  so not only is uncle Ken not a virgin but he is like having crazy ass sex. ahahahaha omg I didn't mean ASS SEX I meant the sex he probably has with ron is crazy-ass . . . but ummmm i guess the other thing isn't exactly a lie . . . ok jane this is when u STOP TALKING.
  Sorry i am like so out of it—I was up all night with my friend bree who gave birth to a baby girl this morning!!!!!!! Her name is kaylinn.
  OMG OMG OMG WAIT!!!! I have told u about Bree! she is that girl I emailed u about from vegas! the one I wanted to hire to take Kens virginity back in the day hahaha. thank god you said no. she doesn't even do that anymore. Now she

works @ the courtyard marriott. anyway we have kept in touch ever since that wknd we hung out in Vegas and she just asked me if I wanna be kaylinn's godmother. I told her yes as long as she promises not to die because u know me I cant even keep a plant alive LOL. Which is ironic cause I am starting to think i might want to be an EMT???!!

Anyway did u write back to Kens email? Should we get him flowers or something? Or wait maybe he will take that as an insult cause its like, HERE YOURE GAY HAVE SOME FLOWERS hahaha. let me know what u think.

Also let me know how u are. last time we talked u sounded really depressed w/ job stuff and feeling like u had wasted your life and were getting old etc. I keep telling u move to Arizona! YOU WOULD LIVE LIKE A QUEEN HERE. Srsly i have so many acres on my property and I work in fucking TJ Maxx. You cd get like a mansion haha. Youd just have to deal with the fact that you would hate all yr neighbors cause they all have guns and I know you are against that big time.

Luv,
Jane

Your Grandma Rose Just Got Your Uncle's E-mail about His Sexuality

Julie, I don't understand the world. Why would my son air his dirty laundry on the computer for everyone to read? At least the news is good. I don't care who that kid goes to bed with as long as it's someone. So I guess it's just regular laundry.

Your Dad Just Learned about Your Uncle's Sexuality from Social Media

Julie,

I noticed on Facebook that my former brother-in-law has decided to spare us any further charades about his sexuality.

Unfortunately, revelations at Ken's advanced age are bittersweet. At fifty-eight, he has somewhere between five and forty years to enjoy an authentic life, depending on his physical health. Given his current BMI, I estimate he will fall on the lower end of that spectrum.

Perhaps this could have been avoided if Ken had been responsive to a leading question I asked him in the late 1980s. While watching the summer Olympics at our house on Hope Street, your uncle compared the diver Greg Louganis to a Greek god. In response, I suggested that Ken too might favor the ancient Greek style of relations. At the time, he was unamused.

It seems now that Ken merely feared my penetrating insight, if you'll forgive the innuendo.

Dad

Your Mother's Goddaughter,
Who Did Everything Right,
Is Feeling a Little Lonely

Hey Julie,

My mom just forwarded me the e-mail from your uncle Ken . . . WHOA.

When I read it, I got so paranoid about all the offensive things we probably said to him when we were little without even realizing it. Like that weekend our parents all went down to DC for the Clinton inauguration and Ken was babysitting us and we made up a multiple-choice survey about sex and pretended it was a homework assignment (even though he knew we didn't go to the same school, so I'm sure he realized that was bullshit). The questions were like, "Check yes if you have ever had sex with a midget."

Jesus, I'm cringing just trying to remember what else we said on that questionnaire. I know I used to call things "gay" and "queer" all the time, so I probably did that. We just had no fucking idea back then. Crazy how different things were not that long ago.

Actually, I guess the '90s were a really long time ago. For some reason, no matter how many years go by, I always think the '90s were ten years ago.

Fuck, when did we get so old?

It just didn't seem like there were a lot of rules about anything back then, you know? And now suddenly there are so many. Obviously I'm biased because I was a kid then and now I'm on the other side, but it just feels like being a parent has gotten insanely complicated. You'll deal with this too whenever you have kids, but I can't tell you how many rules there are—at least in Park Slope. At first I didn't mind because the whole thing was new and exciting and it was like a fun challenge to do everything right, but after a while it gets really exhausting. You just end up constantly being paranoid you're going to fuck something up. Like last month, Aurelia's teacher sent her home because I packed her lunch in a plastic bag and they don't want her setting a bad example for her classmates about the environment. And then a little boy in her class was expelled for sexual assault because he pulled down his pants during recess. And Aurelia's best friend is a little girl named "Woven."

That's not a rule obviously, I just thought you'd find that amusing because you find everything amusing. You know who doesn't find anything amusing? The mothers at a Brooklyn co-op nursery school.

Sorry to vent. I really did just want to respond to the Ken-coming-out thing. Let me know if you ever come through NY—would love to see you. And there's plenty of room for you to crash with us—Kevin's been working really late and traveling a lot, so I'm alone in our place most of the time. I mean, I'm hanging with Aurelia, but it's not like I can talk to her about politics or the sex dreams I've been having about Christoph Waltz (does that make me a self-loathing Jew or what?).

Love,
Rach

PS—Just had another flashback to that weekend when we were little and you came to stay with us when your parents went down

SUSANNA FOGEL

to New York to meet with the adoption agency about adopting Jane. Remember we were obsessed with how they should adopt a "foreign sister" so we'd have to teach her everything about American culture? God, we were such little weirdos!

Your Mom Has Mixed Feelings about the Technological Revolution

Honey,
Thanks for making all the travel arrangements for Ken's wedding using Expedia.com and AirBedandBreakfast.com. I'm glad we'll get a chance to make some new memories in Florida—I still have nightmares about that family vacation we took to Palm Beach right before your dad and I decided to split up. I barely even remember him being there with us, between all his phone calls and his head buried in that computer. This time, we'll all be looking up and around at the beautiful scenery! And I won't have to roast alligator sausages all by myself.

I do have to admit, I felt a little guilty about not using my travel agent for our trip. I've always really liked Roz personally. But as Loni reminded me, this doesn't mean I can't still be friendly with Roz or cohost meet-ups with her for the Democratic Party, like we did during the Obama campaign. And she may not even find out I used the internet to reserve my trip. I was a little concerned she would, because I remember an episode of *Law & Order: SVU* where a male travel agent hacked into all those websites, but in his case he had a sinister plot to figure out where single women were planning to go on their vacations so he could kidnap and sexually abuse them. I think it's safe to say Roz doesn't have any interest in that! And she has a new baby grandson, Ezra, so I would imagine she's (pleasantly) distracted these days.

I've attached a picture of Ezra.

I also wanted to let you know a piece of sad news: Uncle Ken called me last night to say that Ron's family has changed their RSVPs. They won't be coming to the wedding. They're very observant Mormons, as you know, and decided after some hemming and hawing that it would be disloyal to their church to attend the ceremony, since they don't support same-sex marriage. Obviously this is very painful news for Ron, who feels deeply connected to them despite the differences in their religious beliefs. But as he put it himself— being a drama teacher—the show must go on. I told Ken if there's anything we can do to help, just let us know. I'm sure if we all just circle around Ron with our love, he'll feel welcomed into a new family that will support him unconditionally.

On the bright side, I do have some good news to share . . . Loni just helped me hook up "Netflix" for my television! And I still have my cable box. I can't believe how much entertainment is at my fingertips! I just wish I'd gotten around to this earlier, so I could have started working my way through all the programs years ago. I haven't even made it past all the As yet. But I did discover an interesting series from Sweden called *AAAAA14*, about a woman who was cloned in a laboratory. The star of it reminded me of one of the actresses you wrote about last month in your article "Celebs Who Have Sexy Resting Face."

Love,
Mom

Your Dad Discusses the Optimal Family Vacation

Julie,

I enjoyed your piece for the *Huffington Post* on celebrity tattoos. In particular, I appreciated the reference to Norse mythology in discussing Amanda Peet's ankle. Your efforts to make your day job, no matter how unstimulating, at least a little nutritious for the reader are admirable.

I also noticed on your sister's Facebook page that you two are planning to attend your uncle's wedding in Florida next month. You may recall our wonderful family vacation there in the early 1990s. Perhaps it was the fertile vegetation of the Caribbean, but that week was a particularly fertile period for my work as well—it was there that I authored my groundbreaking piece on Tourette's syndrome for the *New England Journal of Medicine.*

To this day, that trip remains one of the more productive vacations I've taken.

Love,
Dad

Your Grandma Rose Is Really Looking Forward to Her Son's Gay Beach Wedding

Julie, I don't know what to pack for Key West. The wedding invitation said "beach attire," but old ladies don't have any of that anymore. We cover up our bods. And you probably heard Ron's family isn't coming at all. Poor kid. I just don't understand the Mormons. What kind of man wants more than one wife? Every man I've met would tell you one is plenty.

Your Mom Just Discovered Breaking Bad

Hi sweetie,

I wanted to thank you for taking the time to call and walk me through how to use Netflix. Now that I think about it, it makes a lot more sense that I shouldn't have to watch hundreds of hours of television in alphabetical order just to get to the program I actually want to watch! I was starting to feel tyrannized!

But the good news is that while I was "in the dark," I discovered a great series. It's called *Breaking Bad*. Have you seen it? It's a story about a high-school science teacher, his relationship with his family, who he cares about very much, and the powerful bond he forms with a younger man from his neighborhood in New Mexico whose parents were not as loving. It's a show about parenthood. Actually, that's not the only focus of the show. There's another big one . . .

The desert scenery. Watching each episode, I couldn't

help but be transported back to my early thirties, when I traveled to New Mexico with Dad, who had a medical conference there. It was just before I discovered I was pregnant with you, and I still remember roaming around Taos, tasting some wonderful green chili, and finding my favorite topaz earrings at a small kiosk. I talked to the shopkeeper for hours about her son, a professional boxer. I also bought a small stone in the shape of my "spirit animal," the badger.

The show touches on some other storylines as well, but I found those less interesting.

I also wanted to let you know that Uncle Ken called me last night to ask a favor regarding his wedding in Florida next month. It's last minute, but Ron's nephew reached out and said he would like to attend after all. He's not sure whether or not he's going to tell his parents, because as you know they are objecting to the wedding on religious grounds. But he has always felt close to Ron and would like to show his support. Ken called to ask if we had any spare room in the AirBedandBreakfast.com we're renting, since the hotels are all booked this late in the game. I told him it's pretty tight quarters, but Ron's nephew is welcome to sleep on the pullout couch. I'm not sure whether he'll take me up on my offer—he might not be comfortable with sleeping in an exposed space with so many women around, given his religion, but I'm not familiar with all the rules. I'm sure he feels the same way about the Jews!

Anyway, I hope it's okay with you and Jane that I offered—I've just e-mailed her too. If you'd like to contact Ron's nephew in advance to introduce yourself, Uncle Ken said he thinks he's on Facebook. His name is Bridger

Jensen, and he's based in Provo, Utah, where he works as a tour guide on hikes and camping trips. He sounds like a very brave and compassionate young man, figuring out which parts of his faith make sense to him and which don't. I'm really looking forward to meeting him.

See you in Key West! I'm already dreaming about which songs by the Four Tops I'm going to request on the dance floor!

Love,
Mom

Your Sister, on Your New Mormon Cousin

UGHHHHHH WHY DOES MOM HAVE TO INVITE A RANDOM JESUS FREAK TO CRASH WITH US?!?!!?

all I have to say is he better not judge me for all the weed I am planning to smoke on this trip lol. srsly im about to spend all my fuckin vacation days for the year and i intend to get my moneys worth! i bet he'll be nice tho cause isn't that like part of their religion? there was this Mormon guy Tad who worked with me at TJ maxx and he was the friendliest fuckin man. he was weird tho—like one time our boss asked him to vacuum and he didn't wanna go into the intimates section so he made me vacuum that area for him! i guess he didn't want to touch the underwear that fell on the floor or something for religious reasons? i was like sure whatever dude I don't really care if god judges me for picking up these fuckin huge purple panties no one wanted to buy in a regular store haha. he ended up moving down to mexico to convert people to his faith or whatever. oh fuck what if ron's nephew tries to do that to us?! watch Mom become a Mormon now haha. that lady is so fuckin obsessed with other cultures.

Your Sister Has an Update about Your New Mormon Cousin

JULES.
I AM AN ASSHOLE.
   im so sorry i didn't get a chance to say goodbye to u before you left for the airport this am!!!!!! I really hope u weren't worried about me bc I didn't sleep @ the condo last night. dont worry I didn't like go home w the caterer or anything. Despite his efforts hahaha
   Actually the reason I didn't come home is more unexpected . . . it has to do with Bridger our new fave Mormon cousin LOL. that sounds bad . . . we just stayed up talking and it wasn't romantic or anything—I don't even think he is allowed to hook up with girls even if he wanted to which is a shame for the women of the world bc did u see his fuckin muscles when he was holding up the chairs for that jewish chair dance?!?! Probably cause the mormons make him like chop logs all day for the temple or whatever . . .
   Anyway i don't think u got much of a chance to talk to Bridger cuz you had yr hands full with mom (omg when she was singin along and dancing to that "aint no mountain high enough aint no valley low enough" song and everyone was like GO BARBARA! GO BARBARA! GO GO GO

BARBARA! bahahahaha). but I was talkin to him in line for the bathroom and told him I liked his speech about ron and we started talking and guess what? it turns out Bridger is also adopted!!!!! We kinda ended up bonding about that bc its like if we had been adopted by other families, our lives wd be so different and maybe we would fit in better (no offense to u obviously u are my bae but u know what i mean . . .).

So yah I guess the wedding was pretty weird for him bc as you know his whole family like refused to come bc they don't approve of homosexuality and Bridger was like, um this is my favorite fuckin person in this family and its legal now federally so who the fuck cares at this point?!! It actually made me appreciate mom and dad for all their craziness cause at least we have never had to deal with them like hating other people for their life choices??? He is just realizing he doesnt see eye to eye with his family as he gets older but he doesn't want to hurt them by like leaving the church or whatever? anyway we were just sitting around on the beach talking (I may or may not have brought a bottle of wine I stole from the bar and drunk it myself bc he doesnt drink LOL) and we ended up falling asleep. nothing else happened but he is a really cool guy and we added each other on FB. it was just one of those random nights where yr like ok maybe not everyone is what I thought!!!!!!!!!!!! LIFE LESSONSSSSSSS

did u have a good time???? i had so much fun dancing with u. OH ALSO at some pt we need to talk about how grandma rose drank like four scotches before her toast and then talked all this shit about mom and dad's marriage! she was all THS IS THE FIRST TIME IVE LIKED

ANYONE A CHILD OF MINE HAS MARRIED. Did u
see mom's face? Shes thinkin like ummmmm wait I am yr
only other child hahaha. oh well sorry dad apparently u did
not make a very good impression on this side of the family!
not that dad wd even care. He'd be like whatever i only care
what chinese people think of me now haha.

Luv u babe!

Jane

Your Grandma Rose Has Been Communicating with Another Dimension

Julie, You should come to visit soon so you can see what
is happening with my little owls. You know I collect things
with owls, like magnets, clocks. When I walk past them
now their eyes follow me, and they watch me in the kitchen.
The big owl clock you got me for my birthday is in charge of
everything and he talks to me while he keeps the time.

Your Sister Thinks Your Grandma Rose Might Be Losing Her Shit

hey dude i just called u but it went straight to vm. did
grandma rose email u about some painting in her apartment that started talking or some shit??? do u think she is
fuckin with us? i mean shes usually funny but shes never
really played a joke like that on us . . .

I kinda think we shd tell mom. i know shes at some Shakespeare festival in vermont with that lady loni and I don't wanna bug her but just in case there is some kind of situation she needs to deal with or whatever? i dunno. i might try to call grandma on my next cig break just to see if shes ok. text me before 5 if u want me to dial u in.

(or maybe rose is just high on some new meds or something in which case she needs to hook a granddaughter up LOL)

Your Mom Has Been Having Some Issues with Regularity

Hi girls,

I'm e-mailing instead of calling because it's after visiting hours in the ICU. Dr. Atay let me stay in Grandma's room an extra hour as long as I promised not to disrupt the patients who are asleep. Hopefully this typing sound won't wake anyone up.

Grandma's doing much better! The medication reduced the swelling in her brain, so she's stopped hallucinating, even though she did ask Dr. Atay if he was part of a government conspiracy. I know she'll be so happy to see you both in the morning. Were you able to get yourselves on a red-eye?

Could one of you also do me a favor? If either of your airports has one of those General Nutrition Center kiosks, could you pick up something for me with buckwheat, bran, or another type of fiber? Tablets are fine, but I prefer a powder I can put in yogurt. I was so distracted when I was

SUSANNA FOGEL

packing, I forgot to bring that Ziploc bag with all my stuff from Whole Foods you girls call my "other purse."

I can't wait to have you two here with me.

Love,
Mom

PS—Julie, Dr. Atay is about your age. I think his family is from Turkey. He doesn't wear a wedding ring, but I haven't been able to get more information because every time I ask about his home life, he suddenly has to go see other patients. Maybe my mom can help us do a little detective work when she wakes up.

The Container of Hummus in Your Grandma's Hospital Room Has Another Take on Suffering

Julie,

I am so deeply sorry. To stand by your grandmother's bedside as she nears death, unconscious for days on end, is purgatory in itself. What profound suffering your family must feel as you gather to remember this matriarch, to honor her memory and her profound impact on those she touched as she prepares to pass to another life.

Also: I can hear your stomach growling from all the way across the room.

You cast furtive glances in my direction, craving my garlicky protein aboard a cracker or baby carrot. Yet, you stop yourself. How can you even think about eating at a time like this? Why haven't you cried yet? Worse still, you were able to sleep a full eight hours last night! Are these not signs that you are heartless, you silently wonder. Surely this is not how one suffers if one truly cares about anyone but oneself and one's own base needs. Surely you are not grieving right. And for that you feel "awkward."

Forgive me, but in the Middle East we do not understand this concept, "awkwardness."

Come; reward yourself for the excellent choice of snack you made when you stopped at Costco on your way to the hospital. I am a versatile spread or dip, centerpiece of so many tables. Family reunions, funerals, fraternity parties, book clubs—name a gathering, and hummus is there! I am, so to speak, the great equalizer. (Ironic, since my origin lies in the West Bank, no?)

Do not get me wrong! I am comfortable here in my perch on the countertop near the medical waste bin, next to your mother's purse (which is itself so capacious that in my homeland one would have assumed it transported several Uzis). From this vantage point I have watched visitors come and go. First, your uncle Ken and his husband, Ron, arrived with small speakers to play the Italian opera your grandmother loved. I watched as Rose, though unconscious, moved her lips as if trying to sing along. Next, your mother's friend from childhood arrived with flowers—Sarah, the one who could be her identical twin. (Though perhaps this is my bias—I must admit I find it difficult to physically distinguish Jewish women in their sixties from one another. But I love them all, just as they love me. In addition to physical likeness, they all share a deep love for hummus.) They laughed through tears, remembering the time Rose forced them to sit inside on a summer day and listen to a lecture on how to do their own taxes so they would never need to depend on a man in financial matters.

And you! Who could doubt that you loved your grandmother? Memories of her will come to you throughout life without any effort at all. This is the nature of grief. It is irrational and haunts us when we least expect it. Perhaps next week, after returning to Los Angeles, you will walk to the Atwater Village Farmers' Market and see a granddaughter helping her grandmother sell candles. Then, your tears may come. Perhaps in five years, you will dream one night that you are at the beach with Rose, only to wake and remember she is gone. Then, to sleep will be impossible. Perhaps in ten, you will vacation in England and plum pie will be on the dessert menu. You will remember it was the only thing Rose ever baked. Then, you will be unable to eat. It is in these moments that we stop thinking of ourselves. They will come soon enough.

Perhaps your sister, Jane, has realized this. As she sits by the window, look carefully in her lap. She is playing Candy Crush. And she may have loved Rose most of all.

Thus why leave me untouched on the counter, only to discard me when you leave for the night because I have been sitting out for twelve hours and technically I do need to be refrigerated?

Peel back my wrapper; do not forsake me.

—Sabra™

Your Dad, Who Never Liked His Mother-in-Law, Just Saw She Died on Facebook

Julie,

I saw on your Facebook page that you lost your maternal grandmother last night. Thank you for tagging me in the photo of all of us on Christmas in the midnineties. Out of respect for Mei-Ling I have removed the tag, but I do remember that day fondly, from the matinee of *Braveheart* to our dinner at Hunan Palace with the Isersons.

As you know, your Grandma Rose and I never saw eye to eye while I was married to your mother. I still believe that had she found a better psychopharmacologist and the right SSRI, she might have had some relief from her petty negativity and rigid judgments. It's unfortunate that she was so resistant to discussing this with me when I would raise the issue at family dinners.

Still, I'm sure she will be deeply missed by some. Please pass along my condolences to your sister as well.

Dad

Your Sister Has an Idea for How to Put the Fun in Funeral

Heya,

Just tried to leave u a voice mail but I think yr phone is dead. Or u are probably busy w/mom helping her make arrangements for the funeral ugh. So sorry to ditch u and put all of that on you . . . my boss is so psycho to make me fly back to Arizona just to work for TWO FUCKING DAYS and then just fly all the way back across the country to say goodbye to my fucking grandmas body. He is such a dick dude. You know this is all bc he tried to bone me when I first started here and i shut that shit down . . . ugh everything that douche does is so fuckin against the law . . .

Anyway i was wondering if u can do me a favor—big surprise cuz i am always asking u for favors haha. do u remember my friend alex from HS who worked at Aaron Bros picture frames? tall with red hair? So he is kinda dealing now and I had asked if he could hook me up with some shrooms when I come back this weekend. I know that sounds weird probably but I did them last fall when I had to put Riley to sleep after he bit that sheriff . . . I went out to the desert with all these pix of us on all of our adventures and his old collar and bowls etc. and did shrooms and just like sat with his memory for a few hours and left all the stuff there and it was like I was laying him to rest in peace in my memory if that makes sense?

U can see where this is going. i wanna do that with grandma rose.

I think Sunday after the funeral I am gunna drive down to the south shore by rhode island where she used to rent that little house and just sit on the beach and like feel allllllllll the feelings ugh. do u wanna come? I am gonna bring all the stuff that reminds me of Grandma, like those ginger snaps she used to buy that i used to hate when I was little then I realized they are actually fucking awesome, and pix of her old house in seattle where she had all those fruit trees and she used to give me rides in the wheelbarrow (I know she used to do that w/you too from your Instagram pix on Throwback Thursday) and that poem she always used to read us about the Jabberwocky.

Ugh fuck im crying even typing this im a fuckin mess. This is hitting me like a ton of fuckin bricks for some reason. Grandma rose was my favorite person in the family except you. and I don't share DNA with any of you but i felt like i had a resemblance to her in personality u know? she was just this no BS awesome fuckin lady.

anyway that's why I wanna do this shrooms thing i think u should join me for. I know u are not really a drug person but this is a special occasion and I really think it would be good for you to get out of your head and we would have this special experience as sisters. Omg I sound like a lifetime movie lol but u know what I mean.

Either way this is where the favor comes in . . . so that dude alex said he has shrooms in stock (haha "in stock" u can tell i have been workin retail too fucking long) and he can hook me up but he has to go to Albany tomorrow afternoon to visit his son (did I tell u he knocked up some randomass woman he met at an Eve 6 concert???) so he would need someone to pick them up before 4 p.m. tomorrow. As u know my flight doesn't get in till like midnight so is there any way u can meet Alex during the day and grab them? he works in dedham in the dunkin donuts at the train station off route 128. He said he will meet u by the commuter rail parking lot. i told him he has to store it in like five containers bc you are fuckin paranoid. text me if u are down and i will give u alex's #

i hope I am not putting u in an uncomfortable situation by asking this!

i also hope u will decide to come to the beach with me sunday. It will be fucking intense obviously but its like whatever we only live once and so did grandma, u know?

Love u girl,

Jane

Ps—mom said Raj asked if he can come to the funeral since he met Grandma when u were together? are u thinking about giving him a second chance? Just be careful boo. I know im the younger one but when it comes to u, I am a fuckin psycho mama bear.

Pps—I am thinking about getting a tattoo with grandmas bday on it. I told mom cause u know she always said to tell her if we ever get tattoos (not that she has any chance of that happening w/ you haha). she was actually cool w/it and I think she was touched, she said just don't get it on my arm cause of the Nazis. Why is everything always about being Jewish with her!!!?!!?

Your Sister, Who Has Two Exes in Jail, Agrees That You Gotta Do You

HEY GIRL HEY

I saw the pic on insta of u givin raj a piggy back ride @ your bday party. first of all how wasted were u hahaha.

anyway im assuming u posted it so everyone cd see that you guys have decided to give it another chance and i just wanted to say i am happy for u. i know I was warning you when he came to grandma's funeral and shit but last weekend this girl at my work's sister came to visit and she gave us these personality tests from a magazine about psychology and she said i need to work on not being so suspicious. so yah. I just wanted to say I respect whatever u choose, especially in this time that has been hard w/grandma dying and you being depressed about turning 34 and not being a real writer yet etc. so whatever makes u feel good I cannot argue with . . . and also guys can change! Like u cant force them to but if its their idea it can happen. Um hello that's how AA stays in business.

Oh and that's a great shirt for yr boobs. Not that I am objectifying my own sister or anything LOL.

x to the izzo,
Jane

Ps—i know im a dick and i didn't get u anything for ur birthday yet but please save this email bc it is officially a coupon for us to get pedicures the next time I come visit you. omg remember when we took mom to get manicures after grandma's funeral to cheer her up and she kept being like DON'T FORGET MY CUTICLES and the manicure lady was like why did I leave Vietnam for this bahahahahaha

Your Mom Can't Help It, She's a Romantic

Honey,

Jane just told me you and Raj got back together—or are in the process of doing so, that a conversation is happening. I won't ask questions about the details of when and how you two made this decision because I don't want to embarrass you, but I did want to send you a note to say how proud I am of you for letting your heart be your guide. One thing I've learned in my years as a psychoanalyst is that people can be very dogmatic and unforgiving when it comes to giving second chances, but the truth about why people are unfaithful is always more complicated, with layers both conscious and unconscious that often have to do with childhood trauma.

In Raj's case, growing up in a predominantly white suburb of Connecticut must have been challenging on a number of levels. He's very lucky to have someone as supportive as you who is so invested in the healing of those wounds. Obviously I've never met that bartender at the Cha Cha Lounge, but I would be surprised if she was anywhere near as empathetic or insightful as you.

I'm keeping my fingers crossed for you two!

Love,
Mom

Your Dad Would Like to Weigh In on a Decision You Already Made

Dear Julie,
I just noticed on your Facebook page that you and Raj have decided to take another stab at a relationship.

Statistically speaking, second chances rarely ever lead to a successful partnership. Most often, the problems and incompatibilities that led to the first breakup resurface sooner or later, despite the initial euphoria of a reunion.

But as Bob Dylan famously said, "You can't be wise and in love at the same time."

Dad

Your Cousin Paul,
Who Has Three Very Expensive Watches,
Actually Did Something Interesting

To my family,

Mass e-mail isn't really my style, but I just wanted to give you all a heads up about something that happened to me recently so you don't read about it in a magazine first. Some of you may have heard about this from my mom already.

Long story short, the investment firm I work for (Prudent Capital) just found out that *Vanity Fair* is going to be running a piece about us in their December issue. It turns out a guy who started working in the mailroom last summer was actually a journalist working on a story about modern hedge-fund culture in New York and decided to do a profile on Prudent because everyone at the company is under forty. Obviously this was a huge violation of everyone's trust, especially my friend Chris's and mine (for anyone who visited me at college, you probably met Chris—he was president of my fraternity), because we really took Evan under our wing and were even starting to groom him to maybe work for us next year. Chris and I take brotherhood really seriously in the real world too.

Anyway, it turns out Evan included a lot of really unflattering details about some things that happened when we were off the clock. Mostly this is just stuff my boss, Dave, did, but there is one detail about me in there too. I'll just come out and say it:

Basically, I smoked crack at my company's Fourth of July party.

Let me just give you the context.

The culture of my company is very dog-eat-dog, especially because of what is going on with the economy right now. If any of you have seen *The Wolf of Wall Street*, we're not that bad, but that is a pretty realistic depiction of the general "work hard, play hard" culture. We spend a lot of weekends at Dave's house in the Hamptons, etc. He calls it "team building," and it's basically a job requirement to go. So when our CEO, Sunil (who is mentioned in the section about tax fraud), told us he'd rented a yacht for the Fourth, we all knew it wasn't optional. Molly decided to stay home because she had just found out she was pregnant (that's the other thing I wanted to tell you, but this seemed more important to get out of the way).

When we got to the party, it was basically the same as it is at work: you do whatever the senior partners are doing or you get hazed. So when Sunil's neighbor from Gramercy Park showed up with some drugs (not a big deal to him because he's an artist and Jackson Pollock's grandson), things went to the next level.

As far as what was going through my head when I made the actual decision to smoke crack, I honestly don't really remember everything from that night because I had been drinking too. That's the other thing—it's not like this was a conscious decision I made. You do **not** have to worry that

I have a drug problem or anything. This was literally the first time I've ever done anything like this. You've all known me a long time and you know I have always been an athlete and my body is my temple. The only substance besides food that I have ever allowed into that temple is alcohol and, when I ran the marathon, Chinese performance-enhancing drugs that were completely legal until last year.

That's why I think what Evan did by lying to us for months is actually worse than what I did: he consciously knew what he was doing. He pretended he was an under-grad from Syracuse wanting advice from Chris and me about the hedge-fund world and asking us to teach him our ways, preying on the fact that our school takes a lot of pride in our alumni network. Now that I know the truth, it makes sense that Evan didn't go to Syracuse. No Orange-man would do what he did.

As for the rest of the article, I also wanted you to know that a lot of sections were exaggerated. For example, the section about hiring Dominican escorts at the cookout on Labor Day weekend to prepare all our meals naked is false.

Yes, we did hire women to help us that weekend, but we did not expect them to get naked.

And just so you know, throughout all this, I have always stayed completely faithful to Molly. She is being a total trouper right now, by the way. FYI just in case any-one tries to contact her and she doesn't respond, she's on a road trip with her friends in her new Range Rover for the next few weeks, but she says she'll be back at the end of the month.

Anyway, that's pretty much it. I just didn't want you to

hear about this from someone else or read the article before I had a chance to get ahead of it. Again, I regret my actions, and if this causes any of you embarrassment or concern, I'm really sorry.

Happy Thanksgiving,
Paul

Your Mother, a Therapist, Gets Why Your Cousin Smoked Crack

Hi girls,

I wanted to touch base about your cousin Paul and what he just revealed in his e-mail to all of us. I can only imagine your shock at learning this new detail, which must seem so inconsistent with the person you thought you knew.

Luckily, you both have a trained psychoanalyst for a mother. I wanted to offer you girls some "words of wisdom" about why Paul's behavior is actually not as surprising as it may seem, at least not from a Freudian standpoint.

I've seen this often in my work among people who grow up in an environment of privilege. Because they are rarely exposed to people of lower socioeconomic classes, they often reach adulthood feeling a subconscious guilt that can be quite overpowering. They struggle with feelings of shame and isolation from the "real world" and yearn to empathize with those less fortunate, to relieve themselves of that burden. They then act out by trying to "walk a mile in their shoes."

In Paul's case, this meant the shoes of the thousands of

underprivileged Americans who are desperate for momentary escape and resort to the use of crack cocaine.

I sent an e-mail to Paul letting him know the real reasons he did what he did. I'm hopeful that when he receives it, he will finally feel understood.

Love,
Mom

Your Sister Is Pretty Excited about Your Cousin's Criminal Activity

OH
MY
GOD
PAUL
WTF

Dude can i just tell u i was in the middle of my shift when I got pauls e-mail and I go HOLY FUCK really loud in the middle of my store then I look over and see that our regional manager is standing right there bc he is in town to do store inspections haha WHOOPS. Anyway I will just keep u posted on whether I still have a job by the end of the day . . . if they fire me I am suing paul for my wages bc he can afford it!

And ugh MOM whyyyyyy does she always have to analyze everyone's secret motivations??!?!?!?!?! Also she is giving paul WAY too much credit. that dude def does not feel guilty about being rich or he would not have gotten married on a fuckin golf course! That kid did crack cause he wants to get fucked up which is the only reason anyone does it including fuckin crackheads! LOL sometimes I just wanna tell mom not everything is a deeper statement about humanity but u know if I did she would just be like HONEY WHAT IS MOTIVATING YOU TO CORRECT ME IS IT BECAUSE OF YOUR TRAUMA haha. OMG I hate when she says TRAUMA, she pronounces it so weirdly! Like TROWWWWWWma hahaha like um where did that accent come from, ancient Germany???

Kk Gotta go back inside and sell some more size 16 pants to the fake housewives of Arizona . . . two more weeks here and then I start EMT training!!!!!!!! Thank fuckin god I am finally getting a life haha.

J

Ps—WHAT IS AUNT ANDREA DOING WITH THIS INFORMATION!?!?!?!?! her skull is def exploding right now . . .

Your Dad, on Your Breakup with Someone He Told You Not to Date

Dear Julie,
I gathered from the recent modifications to your Facebook profile that you and Raj have decided to terminate your relationship again. As you may remember, I predicted this would happen. Maybe next time you'll listen to your old dad when he offers you some wisdom.

You have to think about finding a partner like buying a house, though I realize you are still living in a rented apartment and may not understand the metaphor. A fixer-upper can be a good investment, but only if it has exceptional bones. Raj just isn't a special enough property to justify the hassle and expense of removing all the lead paint.

That said, I understand that breaking up is, as they say, hard to do. Enclosed please find a forty-dollar gift card to Amazon. You may use my Prime account for free shipping.

Dad

Your Stepmother Just Heard about Your Breakup with the Guy You Were Re-dating

Dear Julie,

It is your stepmom, Mei-Ling. Yesterday, your father informed me of your second breakup with your boyfriend, Raj, which would appear to be the Final Solution. (For some reason, your father wishes I do not use this phrase, yet I have no other way to express myself.) While your father holds responsible your careless nature in attempting a reunion with this man, resulting in the passage of precious time, I believe his knee has jerked with this response. In my view, he lacks comprehension of the hearts of women. I have thereby chosen to make contact with you to offer an option that may provide you with comfort: having relations with me.

Before continuing, I wish to caution you that your father knows nothing of this correspondence. As the case is such that my primary hat is that of wife, fierce loyalty to my beloved is of utmost importance. Thus it is my sincere wish that you will benefit from my words herein, but should you inform my other half that I have contradicted him I will have no choice but to claim this letter as a forgery.

I wish to offer first a piece of anecdotal evidence from my life. To put a fine point on it, your father was hardly my first love. That was Jin Jiang, native to Shanghai, who worked for the railroad and bore an impressive stature for a man of Chinese heritage. As a result, he had countless ladies in waiting and a difficulty in committing resembling Raj's. Nevertheless, he declared love for me, donning the label of boyfriend for several years. During this, I allowed him to travel the world unaccompanied and did not compel him to report his whereabouts nor personal encounters. Many friends offered cautionary tales about permitting a man these freedoms, but I solitarily felt that in allowing my beloved to have liberty, I would give him the ability to fly high—though not so high as Icarus, for I felt confident in that he would return to the safety of the nest I weaved. The unfortunate outcome was otherwise. Jin failed at returning, having fallen in love with a server of teas on his train while traversing Russia. To this extent, the very vessel of his freedom became that of his betrayal. My heart burst. Yet after the organic healing of time, I arrived at the conclusion that I did not regret having placed my heart in peril because to experience love is gift in itself, even if the Final Solution is unfavorable.

Thus, I encourage you to pardon yourself for this failed pursuit, removing any whips and chains you may be applying to your own flesh in a metaphorical sense. For to shame yourself for attempting love is to fear life itself and you are no such coward. Our hearts as women bear a striking resemblance to moths within cocoons. They cannot become butterflied prematurely. Perhaps the piece of your heart that remained in Raj's possession during your estrangement had continued to seal your cocoon, preventing you from taking flight. May your pod now open freely, clearing you for takeoff.

Yours truly,
Mei-Ling

Your Dad,
Who Doesn't Understand Your Career Goals,
Just Found Out You Got Fired

Julie,

While sharing my latest haiku on the topic of our country's nuclear-weapons policy on your Facebook wall this morning, I noticed several people in your network had written their condolences. I was able to glean from the text—abbreviations, "frown faces," and all—that the *Huffington Post* has decided to terminate your contract.

Care to tell your dad what happened?

In any case, I would be more than happy to provide cheer in the form of the many reasons I am confident that you are better off not working for that institution. Indeed, I feel it has already wasted years of your time and talent on many levels, and I would love to explain all of them to you in extensive detail.

Give me a call at your convenience—there's more moral support where that came from.

Love,
Dad

SUSANNA FOGEL

PS—If you'd like to call, please wait until after Stuart's violin recital, which should be over at seven o'clock my time. Last time you called, I had forgotten to turn off my phone, and the noise from your call disrupted the concert.

PPS—I noticed you removed my aforementioned haiku from your Facebook wall within seconds. Presumably this is because you disagree that our weapons plan is Draconian. Any interest in debating the point with your old man?

Your Sister, Who Has Been Fired from Five Jobs, Wants to Welcome You to the Club

Hey babes—

I AM SO SORRY I HAVENT CALLED U BACK YET about getting fired!!!!! I suck. im in the middle of my EMT training and they have me on a shift that is 36 hours straight and its fuckin brutal. I am in the van now on my phone which I am not even supposed to be but im pretending its an emergency haha. Which is funny bc when u think about it everything is an emergency in this van!!!!

Anyway I will call u tomorrow but i just wanted to say I cannot believe that fucking happened to you at yr job. So the computer virus made all your private chats visible to yr boss? Like every time we bitched about our jobs online on FB or email or gchat???? That's my fuckin worst nightmare. And it so SUCKS that it was the day Ariana Huffington (sp?) was in the office!!!!!!!! Was she the one that fired u? Ugh.

I told Mario who drives the EMT van what happened

and he said maybe it was a conspiracy by the Govt??? He said they are always tracking every citizen so ppl probably knew about all yr chats before the computer thing even happened????? Mario is really smart—if u want to talk to him he can give u more information about what he knows . . .

On the bright side maybe now u will have more time to work on yr book!!!!! U were just telling me how u were always too tired after work and it made u have writers block so maybe everything happens for a reason. Let me know if u wanna come down here to AZ to clear yr head and get inspiration for yr writing. U are welcome to take my Jeep while im at work and drive up to Jerome for the day which was like an old town of prostitutes from the 1800s or something???? Lol but srsly every time I get fired I go up there to think.

Like when I got fired from that fuckin job at the bathing suit store. Sorry but how was I supposed to know that woman put on five bikini bottoms and walked out of the store? Did u want me to x-ray peoples vaginas when they walk out of there? Broke ppl are fucking sneaky! That's how they survive . . .

Gotta go b/c we are pulling up to a Sizzler where this old lady collapsed. I hope she is still breathing. Ugh this job is so fuckin intense sometimes but Im glad I can make ppl feel better when they are scared.

Also I attached a pic to make u smile in spite of this. As u can see its obviously a baby porcupine drinking a 40 hahaha

Luv
Jane

Your Mom Secretly Kind of Loves
That You're Having a Meltdown

Hi honey,

You have nothing to apologize for. I loved our phone call on Mother's Day. Just because it's a holiday that's supposed to be about me doesn't mean your life is going to stop, or that you can't tell me things that are going on in your life that are painful or traumatic for you. I don't need to be coddled or protected! Maybe some other mothers would, but I'm an incredibly strong person.

I've been thinking a lot about what you were saying—how lately, you've been wondering if you should have done something else with your life and you wonder if it's "too late." First of all, honey, it's not over yet! It's just beginning! It sounds like you're almost done with your book and you just have to get over this "hump." Of course, I understand why you might feel that way sometimes, especially when so many of the people around you have taken a more conventional path. But those people might never know the kind of passion you do. Look at Rachel. I don't get the impression that she's ever been passionate about PR, but she has a nice house and a comfortable life and that's what was most important to her. Or maybe she didn't feel like she could take a risk because Deborah is always talking about how she expects Rachel to take care of her financially after she retires. Aren't you glad I don't put those kinds of expectations on you?

But believe me, I understand how hard it is to feel good about your choices when you're worried about money. As you know, I grew up in a family that had very little. It felt like we were in a constant state of stress. Grandma Rose always used to tell Ken and me, "The point of having money is not having to worry about money."

Which brings me to the other thing I wanted to say—and I can feel Grandma Rose smiling down on me as I type this!—I want to wire you some of the money she left me in her will so you can have a little reprieve from the stress and finish your book over the next couple of months worry-free.

I'll be sending you enough so you can also freeze your eggs if that's something you decide you want to do (I know you mentioned having children briefly on our call as something you feel "behind" on). I hope you don't think this is me putting pressure on you—I'm not like Deborah, who's been telling Rachel she wants grandchildren since Rachel got her first period! Not literally, but you get my point. I have a hunch that this factored into Rachel's decision to get engaged to Kevin after dating him only a short time. I think I mentioned on the phone that they've entered couples therapy. Please don't mention to Rachel or Deborah that I told you that, if you talk to them.

And of course if spending the money that way doesn't feel right to you, that's fine too. I just want you to feel that you have options in your life, and if this would relieve some of the pressure you feel to "figure things out" and would open you up to new experiences and new people, without feeling any sort of "time line," I consider that a very wise investment!

Either way, I'm very grateful we now have the technology that allows women to make these kinds of choices in their lives. It reminds me of Kristina (my friend from Healthworks who is transgender). Maybe the next time you visit home, if you do go ahead with any sort of fertility procedure, you and Kristiña could grab a cup of coffee at Peet's and talk about your experiences. I was telling her about you and she said you sound very funny.

(Apparently she is having trouble making friends in the transgender community with a sense of humor.)

Sending a big hug and a kiss,

Mom

Your Great-Great-Great-Great-Grandmother from Prussia Has a Question about Your Priorities

Shayna maidel,

Not to worry. The rest of this letter will be in English, expertly translated from the Yiddish by yours truly. If you wish to educate yourself, *shayna maidel* means "pretty one." You probably didn't know that because your idea of Judaism is fasting for half a day on Yom Kippur and making an exception for coffee. And in truth, the only reason you fast at all is because you always have a little extra flesh that time of year from drinking too much beer on "Labor Day."

Let me tell you something, *printsesin*. In the old country, every day was Labor Day.

I should introduce myself. I am your great-great-great-great-grandmother Manya Strauss (1804–1854). Impressive, I know. To live half a century was no small feat in those days! Especially in East Prussia, with our endless winters. Now East Prussia is nothing. Pfffft. A place that no longer exists.

You will never know that feeling. Your country is immortal. You will never disappear because today's world records every life, even the women's. Who remembers the life of any woman from my day? Our destiny was merely to reproduce.

But is it yours? Two hours ago, I watched from on high as you and your *zaftig* friend with the too-short dress visited a doctor who is an expert on matters of womanhood (how easy he has it! In my day, he would also have been responsible for calming scarlet fever and performing amputations!). Both of you hoped he could tell you the odds that you can still conceive at age thirty-five and beyond. You left the office with pamphlets about "freezing your eggs," which you now read together in a café as you share a meal you refer to as "brunch" (this we certainly did not have in the old country! Nor did I ever have the luxury of tasting champagne mixed with orange juice!). Your friend with the ample bosom confesses she is desperate to bear children—probably so she can put those milk pails to good use!

You are not so sure. Week after week I have watched you confess this to the analyst you pay handsomely to diagnose your pathologies. Despite the fact that you are practically the age of a grandmother in my day, you feel you have much left to accomplish. You have yet to write something truly memorable. You have yet to travel to three of the world's continents. Though occasionally you yearn for companionship, you enjoy living alone. You wring your hands on Dr. Fleming's couch, wondering if you are broken for diverging from the path women have followed since time immemorial. Pfffft! Those women simply had no choice. The question of children was one I was never asked. My haunches were made to breed. Not that they were shabby, my haunches. Nor was the rest of my body. How many "Pilates" classes did I take to make that happen? Zilch! Life was my Pilates. You waste your money on nonsense. I'll tell you how to tone your mid-section: sleep on a cold wooden floor in East Prussia for ten years because your brothers get the only beds. It's strong triceps you want? Churn butter and whip cream with your bare hands until your wrists swell to the size of rolling pins. For a muscular backside, squat on and off a pail and try to keep your balance while your crazy goat kicks for your head!

Would I have borne children if I had had the choice now at your fingertips? My truest answer is no. My sons were very annoying, as was the duty to service my husband in bed. Nothing personal—he was a wise man who made beau-tiful shoes. But I could not care less about men, their egos, or touching their tiny *schvantzes*. The only person whose body I cared to see was off limits except in my dreams: my best friend from the village. Her name was Shira, and her father grew sugar beets.

That is the other thing. There wasn't even a word for "lesbian" in my day.

What would I have done with your freedoms? Perhaps gone on the road, peddling my wares. What wares? My sense of humor, for which I was known in my village (and for which you are known in your family—you get it from me!). Your son is dying of rubella? Fetch Manya; she'll make him chuckle as he gets ready to meet his maker. Whooping cough your wife's plight? Ask Manya to do her impression of Otto von Bismarck. Your wife will be losing her breath for more reasons than one.

This I also envy about your time. Such wealth can be achieved by a funny woman! If I were alive today, I would surely enjoy the fortune of Lena Dunham.

But although you have not achieved her level of success and almost certainly never will, you have a certain spark, as I did. And so, *shayna maidel*, I beg of you: live your truth as I could not. If it fulfills you to nurture a child, then that is your destiny. If you prefer to live a life of adventure and fulfill your baser needs with casual encounters, that destiny is equally worthwhile. You have only yourself to answer to. Who else would judge an authentic life? Except possibly your friend with the ample bosom, who seems to have judgments about everyone, including many suitors she has never met but views pictures of on her miniature telephone.

Just know that whatever you choose, the world will continue to turn. And whatever you choose, in the end you will end up here with me, laughing together as we spy on all the world's hypocrisies.

Love,
Your Great-great-great-great-grandma Manya

PS—Did your friend with the ample bosom just request that the waiter not bring her any bread with her meal? This, I cannot comprehend. Who turns down an offer of bread?

Your Sister in Arizona Recommends Fried Food

Hey bae mom just told me what happened with yr egg freezing and said you had to spend the night in the hospital with
some kind of uterus infection????? ugh that SUUUUUCKS.
at least yr goin home today so u get to sleep in yr own bed
and be comfy. i wanna come see u but i friggin cant bc i have
my final EMT exam in 2 days (can you believe Im gonna be
saving peoples lives now? something is seriously wrong
with this world lol).

    i wanna come after tho. i can pay for my own tix this
time cuz i have a little left over from grandmas will even
after using most of it for school since im a responsible adult
now (ha yeah right). anyway I wanna do something for u
cause ur my girl and u have had my back over the years in
more ways than one . . . so check yr email. u should find a
gift certificate to california pizza kitchen. remember you
took me to the one near mom's house after we went to the
clinic for my abortion (ummmmm i REALLY hope no one
is reading over your shoulder right now!!!) and we got like
3 orders of that spinach and artichoke dip? i know you
cant put spinach artichoke dip on your uterus haha but i
speak from personal experience that shit is straight up
crack and you will forget you even have a uterus ☺ love
you chica.

One of the Eggs You Just Froze Has a Question

Dear—

Wait, okay, how do I address this letter? Who are you now exactly, in relation to me? 'Cause I was a part of you for thirty-five years, right? We were one. So does that mean I'm addressing this letter to myself? No, because I live in a freezer now and you don't. So I guess you are a "you" now, and I am a "me." But like, what's my age? Am I still thirty-five, like you? Do I continue to be thirty-five until you defrost me? And if we're going with that theory for a second, and I have temporarily stopped aging for the duration of the time that I am in this freezer and therefore I am currently in a state of suspended existence, does that mean I have temporarily ceased to exist?!

As you can tell, I'm freaking the fuck out in here.

Not that that's your problem! Do your thing. No, I just figured I'd touch base to see whether you had a sense of a timeframe for all this. Like if you had to predict how long you'll be keeping me on ice—so to speak—what would you say? Just a guesstimate is fine. 'Cause I remember that one time you and your two best friends went up to that cabin for Becca's thirtieth birthday, and after rewatching all four seasons of *Friday Night Lights* and lamenting that you'd never meet husbands like Coach Taylor, you made a promise that if you got to thirty-eight and were still single, you'd all move to Portland and live in a big Craftsman like hippies and raise sperm-donor babies together and find random lovers to fulfill your sexual needs at night. Are we still on schedule for that? So, T minus three years, you think? Or are you rethinking that whole plan, since Becca got married (I think she settled, by the way) and Taryn's bathroom is always disgusting?

'Cause I know there have also been some conversations with Dr. Fleming lately where you've admitted you're not sure parenthood is right for you at all and you're worried you're just doing this because of societal expectations and both your parents' constant mentions of grandchildren, and she said you have to live your truth. I don't know what that means to you, but I'm guessing it means I may never get out of here—or at least that that's a possibility. Again, no judgment if that's what you choose. Totally get it, totally support it. I'd just personally love to know what to expect. I'm not a fan of surprises in general. They make me very nervous. I have a lot of nervous energy to begin with, and then you add a surprise to the mix? *No bueno.*

Not that it's terrible in here or anything! It's more just a personal preference. I've never really been great with small spaces, and the climate is far from ideal. As you know, I'm used to more of a tropical environment: warm and wet. Oh, God, that sounded disgusting. I'm not trying to be disgusting. I'm just stating the facts about your ovaries, not body shaming you. I would never do that—I have so much respect for women. Obviously; I was inside one for thirty-five years. Not in a sexual way! Well, actually, sort of. God, everything I say sounds disgusting now. And confusing. I'll wrap this up.

So, yeah, just respond at your leisure. Hopefully that won't be too long, but again, it's not about me. You go, girl! I'll be fine in here.

Just circle back to me sooner rather than later if you can. And happy Valentine's Day.

Sincerely,
?????

Your Mother's Goddaughter, Who Chemically Straightened Her Hair for Years, Now Appreciates Your Freak Flag

Jules—

We made our flight! Whew. Now enjoying my second glass of white wine and the free Wi-Fi . . .

I just wanted to thank you again for this weekend. I really needed to get away from New York for a couple of days. Aurelia had the best time—she will not stop talking about Legoland. And I'll never forget her throwing up on the street outside the Scientology Celebrity Centre and that guy screaming at her from inside.

I <u>really</u> think that was the guy from *NCIS*.

Also . . . I decided to move forward with the divorce. I really appreciate you letting me talk through it and not judging me for being a sobbing mess and drinking all your beer (Trader Joe's Ale=not terrible! Who knew?). You're totally right, all that matters is what makes me happy, and seriously, who gives a shit what anyone else thinks? (Including my mom, but don't tell her or your mom I said that . . .)

And hang in there with all your stuff. I didn't realize you

were having such a hard year. That's a lot to deal with: the breakup, getting fired, freezing your eggs. It sounds like one of those times in life where the universe just takes a huge shit all over you. But I really think things are about to turn around for you. I mean, you just finished a <u>book</u>—that's huge.

Okay, I should probably go be a good mom now (just looked over and realized the man sitting on the other side of Aurelia is watching a movie with a sex scene and my daughter is staring at it, mesmerized . . . whoops). I'll let you know how things go with Kevin. And keep me posted on what publishers say about your book.

If I don't see you before then: will you be back in Boston for Passover? If so, let's ditch our moms and go shopping on Newbury Street or something.

Love,

Rach

PS—Re: the gift card I left for you, I'm not assuming you still shop at Bath and Body Works or anything—just thought it was a fun throwback ☺

Your Emotionally Withholding Dad Just Heard about Your Recent Success!

Julie,

I talked to your sister today and she passed along the news that you have sold your first manuscript as a professional writer after many years of struggling.

You need to invest at least a portion of what you net into a money-market account. If you don't put your earnings somewhere where they can accrue interest, you are essentially throwing money down the toilet, and then you'll be back to square one.

Why didn't you tell me the good news right away?

Dad

Your Mom Thinks Jane Fonda Is Very Inspiring

Dear Julie,

I can't tell you how excited I am for you that your hard work has paid off! What an honor to know your work will be published for the whole world to read (do you know yet if there will be any foreign language translations? If so, I'll buy them all, and take a "crash course" in the various languages so I can follow along). Not that there was any doubt in your mind (at least, I hope there wasn't!) about this, but I could not be prouder to be your mother.

Loni wanted me to tell you congratulations too. She also asked me if I planned to "tweet" the good news about your book. I told her I didn't think so, but I wasn't sure what she meant by that.

I have some good news too. Believe it or not, it has to do with technology. Have you heard of something called a "pod cast"? At first I was afraid to try it because I thought it involved something with time travel. Then I found out it's just a tape on the Internet. Inside each pod is a story or interview. One interview in particular really inspired me.

SUSANNA FOGEL

It's with a famous woman I always knew of but never knew much about. Now, after listening to this woman speak so eloquently in the pod, I feel like I've known her forever . . .

I'm talking about Jane Fonda.

As I'm sure you know, Jane Fonda was a real icon in my generation, both for her beauty and for her acting. What you might not know is that lately she has expanded her repertoire to become an activist for feminism and other causes. One thing Jane Fonda talks about inside the pod is how it's much harder for women to find companionship after a certain age than men. Jane Fonda herself has spent most of her life after fifty being unmarried. Meanwhile, she points out that men don't have the same struggle to find new partners after divorce, no matter how old they are. Obviously, I agree. Just look at your dad! He found a new partner almost immediately, even though he's incredibly difficult to live with. Of course, it's possible his wife doesn't realize that because of the language barrier.

Loni and I agree with Jane Fonda that this is an injustice. We talked about it a lot last week as we drove home from the Williamstown Theatre Festival. (By the way, Matthew Perry was fantastic—it was as if he originated the role of Hamlet!) We stopped in the town of Lee for a bite to eat at a café we had read about in the *Zagat Guide* that blends English country cooking with Thai spices—I think they call that type of combination "diffusion." There we were, sitting on a balcony overlooking beautiful rolling hills dappled with the summer sun. A small duck pond lay in the distance, with a chorus of mallards quacking. As we ate wonderful coconut-curry scones fresh from the oven, Loni turned to me and asked, don't you wish we could grow old here? In that moment, I couldn't help but remember Jane Fonda's words. There are so many chapters in a woman's life that remain unwritten. And so I turned to Loni and said, why can't we? By the time we returned to Brookline, we had decided to sell our condos and buy a house together.

I hope you're not sitting there wondering if your mom has lost her marbles. Quite the opposite! I have never felt clearer than I do right now—it's as though I'm "returning to my roots," taking risks in my life, like I did when I was still in school and traveled all over Europe by myself, before I met your father and life took me in a more traditional direction. That's not to say I didn't enjoy all the pleasures of my life raising you and your sister—and even certain aspects of my marriage to your dad, especially early on. But like Jane Fonda, I have never been a conventional woman at heart. And I won't be taking this leap alone. I have a partner on this journey: someone who has been a wonderful companion to me for the past few years.

(Of course, when I use words like "partner" and "companion" to describe my relationship with Loni, I mean them in a metaphoric sense. There has never been anything physical between us. But I'm not ruling anything out! As Jane Fonda says, life is long . . .)

I know this is a lot to process. I just wanted to tell you as soon as I could. It didn't feel right to have this secret bursting out of me and not be sharing it with my girls. I just sent a similar e-mail to your sister as well. Just give me a call when you have a chance.

SUSANNA FOGEL

In the meantime, maybe I'll send you a copy of this "pod cast" for your birthday!

Love,

Mom

PS—Even though you're not familiar with my new "neighborhood," I want you to feel free to use my new house as a home base. Jane Fonda talks a lot about how important it is to make sure your children feel like they still have a mother, even when they're adults. She talks to each of her children all the time. Her son, Troy, is an actor on a show on HBO about football players called *Ballers*, which sounds very interesting.

Your Sister, Who Works in Retail in Arizona, Has to Tell You about Kimmel *Last Night*

HEY FAMOUS WRITER SISTER ARE U THERE I GOTTA TALK TO UUUU
Ugh OK I guess you just left your chat window open. fuck my shift is starting in a minute so i will just leave this message here and u can catch up whenever u get back . . .

So I was watchin Kimmel last night cuz as u know I fuckin love that man, and he had this dude on his show who just sold his company for 40 million dollars and it's a company that comes to yr house and gives u massages?!?!?! Ummmm is that the dude Grandma Rose set u up with? The one u slept with even though u werent attracted to him but u drank way too much then and u were like what the fuck am I doing and then he flipped his shit on you???

Well ummmmm u should watch this interview cause I think u are mentioned in it?? He kept talkin about how women have never appreciated him but now theyre all gunna be sorry cuz hes so rich and he told Kimmel this story about how he once let his grandma set him up and the girl like led him on? He's all, watch Jimmy now shes gunna be like blowin up my shit. And Kimmel was like should we call her? Let's get her on the phone right now!!!! And I was like OMFG my sisters voice is about to be on national television!!!!!! But then he said he deleted yr number.

wait actually . . . if u do watch this interview I am just warning u that he tells jimmy kimmel you had hairy nipples. U should just know that. i was like oh whatever dude u still fuckin stalked her so obviously it didn't bother u at the time!!!!! and whatever he has crazy eyes. I kept remembering yr story about how u woke up in his house and everything was made of fuckin steel and leather like he was a criminal on one of those fucked up shows mom watches where dudes chop up women (btw why does our mother watch that shit again lol??? that lady is seriously disturbed).

u should email that dude and tell him he should be thanking u right now cuz obviously the only reason he is so successful now is bc he had a taste of yr sweet sweet lovin hahaha. u shd put this on yr dating profile. Like hey boyz if u sleep with me U WILL BECOME A FUCKING MILLIONAIRE. Like in OMG whats the name of that fairy tale about the King that everything he touched turned to gold . . . oh ya Midas!

U HAVE THE MIDAS VAGINA!!!!!!!!!!!!!!!!!!!!!!!!!!!

O fuck im gonna be so late gotta run. Call me when u get this—I also have to tell u how I got this racist asshole at my work fired.

XXXXXXXX

Your Dad's Friend
Who Makes You a Little Uncomfortable
Always Knew You Could Do It

Dear Julie,

I saw your dad today on the mainland, while attending the *New England Journal of Medicine*'s annual awards ceremony (I was honored for my research on the suicidality risks of Accutane). He told me the good news about finding a publisher for your first book!

I'd be a liar if I said I didn't see this coming. I knew you had the talent and dedication, and that it was just a matter of time before the whole world saw in you what I always have.

I'm sorry it hasn't worked out for us to get together any of the times I've been in California over the past few years (now I see what you were always so busy with!), but the next time you're home visiting your parents, drop me a line. I'd love to celebrate with you. I always have business in Boston I can attend to with some advance notice, and there's no better way to toast professional success than with Misquamicut oysters at the Charles Hotel's bar, Noir.

In fact, I'm sitting there right now with a crisp glass

of 2004 Laurent-Perrier Alexandra Rosé and the latest *Harper's*, and I'm raising my glass to you.

With admiration,
Larry Shepherd

Your Sister, Who Has a Career Now, Is Freaking the Fuck Out on the Job

JULIE OMGOMGOMG I JUST GOT THE EMAIL FROM ALITALIA AIRLINES!!!!
ARE U SURE ABOUT THIS!!!!?!?!???

Dude for real tho this is like the nicest thing anyone has ever done for me. U do NOT have to do this just bc I got my EMT certificate! I mean I know its also to celebrate yr book but . . . ugh I feel bad I never do anything for you!!!!!!!!!!

Hahaha anyway I am so fucking touched that u want to spend part of yr book money on this! Srsly I just cried when I opened this email and everyone in the EMT van thought I was upset bc we just watched this old dude die after he hit a tree with his car and I had to be like, um oh no actually I was just crying tears of joy bc my sister is super famous now and wants to take me to Italy for a week to fuckin enjoy life? Which this old man no longer has???? ugh I'm such a little bitch how did I even pass my exam in the first place hahaha mysteries of the universe.

So I guess we will be going to the airport straight from Moms house after Thanksgiving! OMG watch she is gonna try to come with us in our suitcases . . . But I agree with u that we shd ask her to give us a list of all the places Grandma

Rose talked about from when she lived there so we can go. In other news we all know Grandma Rose loved wine so we will definitely be drinking a shit ton of that in her honor! Hahahaha

Thank u so much dude. Im soooooo fuckin proud of u too. I know how hard u have been working for this and I am glad u will get a chance to finally relax for a second!

I LOVE YOU,

Jane

Ps—Do I need a passport to go to Italy? I don't think I have one!

Your Mom's Rabbi's TV Show May Actually Become a Thing

Dear Julie,

I am reaching out as the coordinator of television drama at ShondaLand to let you know that our company will officially be moving forward with *Untitled Rabbinical School Drama*, created by Rabbi Josh Salz. Rabbi Josh approached me with the concept over the high holidays last fall, as my parents are also members of his congregation (I grew up in Needham), and Shonda felt his idea fit perfectly with our company's mandate to combine groundbreaking racial diversity, political commentary, and positive examples of modern women exercising their liberated sexuality in worlds where we've never seen that before, like the infant ICU or the White House Situation Room.

This e-mail serves to confirm that you have no legal

claim regarding *Untitled Rabbinical School Drama*. Rabbi Josh mentioned he was briefly in contact with you two seasons ago, but that you did not develop the project in any way or offer any helpful feedback. He forwarded your brief e-mail correspondence to our legal counsel to confirm that none of your notes were incorporated into our pitch. Our decision to remove the threesome from the episode where Rabbi Jake counsels survivors of a school shooting was due to the fact that we have a similar story line in an upcoming episode of *How to Get Away with Murder* and completely unrelated to your suggestion that there was a tone problem.

Do not hesitate to contact our legal department if you have any questions, but please do not contact ShondaLand attempting to submit your work for future employment. We do not accept unsolicited submissions.

Sincerely,
Jordan Sokoloff
(Dictated but not read)
Coordinator, TV Drama
ShondaLand

Your Mom Finished Reading the Book You Based on Your Family

Julie,

I only have a minute, so I'll make this quick. Loni and I are about to go into town to the farmer's market, and we often find ourselves getting lost there for hours tasting the various cheeses and jams. Today, we have the important task of outfitting our guest bathroom with toiletries, so we will be spending most of our time at the kiosk of a wonderful local woman with very long gray hair. She calls herself S, but I'm not sure what that stands for. She makes her hand soap out of recycled bottles. I'm not sure exactly how one does that, but she offered to give us a demonstration today, provided that she is able to get her son to come help her out at the stand. I've seen her son there with her a couple of times. Sometimes he brings his fiddle to the market, but he never turns his case over to collect money. He just plays for the love of music. I'm not sure if he's your "type," but maybe when you come for Thanksgiving we'll take a walk down there and you can see what you think.

But for now—I just had to let you know that Loni and I printed out your book and stayed up late last night reading the whole thing. We both thought it was fabulous! You've always had such a vivid imagination, creating entire worlds and characters out of thin air. Like the character of the mother who is always claiming she wants to lighten her daughter's load while subtly piling on more burdens. She is just so over the top! It's almost like she's an allegory for something grander, possibly even biblical. She was probably my favorite character, even though I personally related to the others much more. Maybe when you visit us at Thanksgiving, you can tell us where you got the idea to write about someone like that.

One last thing before I forget: it turns out Carly Simon is going to be performing at the Cultural Arts Center in Lenox the day after Thanksgiving. I think she may have some family around here she's planning to spend the holiday with. I hope it's okay with you and Jane that we bought tickets for everyone. We wanted to check first, but it was very early in the morning and we didn't want the tickets to sell out. We had a great time waking up at dawn to go down to the box office—I remember storming the gates of Madison Square Garden for Joni Mitchell tickets in college!

Okay, the natives are getting restless. By that I mean Loni is ringing the bell on her bike basket. Did I tell you we bought bikes? I guess what they say is true—you never forget how to ride. You just have to get back up on one and try.

> With galaxies of love,
> Mom

Your Sister Finished Reading
the Book You Based on Your Family

Bahahahaahahahahahahaahahhahahahahah this shit is amazeballs.

Ok I have to admit i was a little nervous when u said u were writing a book about yr family cause i was like, what if i come off like some fuckin scrub-like bastard sister u never wanted to adopt or something . . . dunno why i thought that—it's not u it's me—but damn i guess i need some more self esteem cause I come off awesome if i do say so myself!!! also thx for changing the names of some of the dudes (and um, one woman) whose hearts I broke over the years. always good to protect the innocent LOL.

ok and um speaking of loveeeeeeeee . . . i have some news. im kinda bringing a dude home for thanksgiving . . . and u have actually met him. ok remember uncle ron's nephew bridger who shared our condo in key west? so last week he was driving thru AZ on his way to cali (he is moving there to work for a construction company) and texted me about having lunch . . . long story short we did not leave my house all weekend haha. i guess he kinda had a religious crisis sparked by that whole fucked up thing with his family about his uncle being gay and totally left the church???? then i guess he spent a year boning his way thru Utah LOL gotta make up for lost time!

anyway yah so his family doesn't really talk to him anymore which sucks but hes doin ok. he just didn't have any thanksgiving plans so i invited him to come with me to Moms weird house in the middle of nowhere haha. he'll just fly home when we go to Italy. I haven't told mom im bringing him yet but u know her, she'll be all EVERYONE LETS ALL GIVE THANKS FOR HOW BRAVE BRIDGER IS FOR LISTENING TO HIS HEART. this time u have to talk to him more—hes so fuckin smart and sweet and just like a good person I dunno. before he left he asked if he could come with me in the ambulance for my shift just out of curiosity and we had to pick up this tiny baby after she fell out of her crib and the way he was holding her and talking to her i was like awwwwwww and then i was like uh oh jane u are so fucked.

K I gotta go shove some food in my face now and work a night shift. cant wait to see u next week at moms—how much do we wanna bet mom and loni have started sleeping together? JK omg i just gagged from that thought, so much for having dinner right now.

Wait omg dude WHAT DID MOM SAY ABOUT YOUR BOOK? Did u show it to her yet?! I just thought about that. um, are u even still invited to thanksgiving?!?!?! hehe if so i will see u there.

congrats again boo. u fuckin nailed it.

love,
jane aka "JENNIFER"

Your Dad Finished Reading the Book You Based on Your Family

Julie,

I read your book. It's a decent first draft (I assume this is a first draft). I did see a lot of places where you could improve the story and hone your comedy to turn what are now chuckles into guffaws. I jotted down a few notes that should be helpful. As you may remember, I contributed to my college humor magazine, so I'm very familiar with what makes for effective satire.

Page 1—I wouldn't go so far as to refer to the patriarch of the story as in the "twilight" of his life. At sixty-five, unless he has Stage IV cancer or its equivalent, he could have up to thirty-five years left to live.

Page 16—You reference the father's affinity for collecting *maitake* mushrooms and mention his trip to Santa Fe. *Maitake* do not grow in the American Southwest. Any editor or publisher who is also a mycology hobbyist will immediately question your authorial voice—unless, of course, you deliberately intend to signify to the reader that you are an unreliable narrator.

Page 43—The mother's expectations of the father seem very unreasonable to me. Is it your intention to cast her as an antagonist?

Page 84—You refer to the parents' adoption of the younger sister as a "desperate, futile attempt on behalf of [the parents] to save their marriage, which cursed her with a childhood of feeling like she never quite belonged; she would spend the next twenty-five years chasing a sense of security through toxic relationships with older men." This makes no sense.

Page 104—Your use of anthropomorphism (i.e., the talking treadmill) raises too many questions, though I applaud your attempt to be Kafkaesque. In your text, the treadmill has a nuanced understanding of human behavior and the pain of existence, but the reality is that even the most advanced robots do not have the ability to empathize. I've attached a link to a recent study from MIT that I contributed to, which outlines the basics here. If you have any more questions about emotional robots, I hope you'll consider me an expert.

Page 145—This is actually more of a general note on tone. Perhaps you are aiming for hyperbole, but the narrator makes some extremely destructive choices when it comes to her love life. I would rethink this given the current conversation around feminism and the Bechdel test (I actually had an idea for a similar test years before, but was met with resistance due to my own gender). Specifically, here you have a female character who is allegedly intelligent very much fitting the trope of the pathetic woman attempting to find herself through bad patterns of dating unavailable men. At the very least, for authenticity I would trace the origin of her issues to a fractured relationship with her father.

Page 168—I found liking the character of Grandma Violet to be a Sisyphean task, to say the least. I would caution you not to assume we will find her to be a sympathetic character just because she narrowly escaped the Holocaust.

Page 179—You overuse the comma.

Page 192—This is a section where you could beef up your jokes. For instance, you refer to the mother character in later life as "a woman Dianne Wiest might have played in a 1980s Woody Allen comedy set on the Upper West Side." Might I suggest replacing Dianne Wiest with Diane Ladd? Much funnier!

Page 204—I would set the "meet cute" between the father and his Vietnamese second wife in another location. The whole massage-parlor bit feels like it's been done.

Page 242—The narrator's ambivalence about having children reads as implausible and off-putting, as does her resentment of the fact that society shames women for being ambivalent about motherhood.

Page 274–290—This was a stretch where I actually had very few notes! Maybe it's because you finally turned your lens on the father's early years, which are incredibly compelling. This was probably my favorite section of the book.

Page 300—As you conclude the story, I found myself

SUSANNA FOGEL

frustrated with the number of loose ends that remain in the narrator's life. Unmarried, childless, with scant savings and no assets beyond a hybrid car—is this really a heroine readers will relate to? I suppose only time—and ideally a vigorous push and marketing campaign from your editor—will tell. That said, anything you might do to increase your "antiheroine's" likability certainly couldn't hurt.

That's all for now. I'm sure as you hone the manuscript I will have more specific notes.

Also, please call me at your convenience to discuss travel plans for Thanksgiving. Mei-Ling and I would appreciate it if you and Jane could arrive in Boston in time for dim sum at 10:30 a.m. on Thursday, before you head to your mother's for more normative holiday fare and then on to Italy. Allow extra time to get to the airport, as we are on a tight schedule; if you miss your flight like last year, your goose will be cooked.

That said, Mei-Ling and I plan to serve goose as an entrée. Let me know if you have any dietary restrictions.

Love,

Dad

Acknowledgments

I owe a massive debt to my incredible agent, Monika Verma, at Levine Greenberg Rostan, who spent two years becoming a multihyphenate in my life (agent-sister-friend-drinking buddy-confidante-wing woman). From our first overly formal lunch where I was intimidated by her tasteful, patterned blouse, to the final edit, when our shorthand had evolved to include emojis and YELLING FEEDBACK OVER TEXT, I would and could not have done this without her.

I'm also so thankful for the team at Henry Holt, for encouraging me to lean into the emotional undercurrents lurking in my comedy. My wry, whip-smart editor, Serena Jones, always made me feel I was in capable hands, and like I was a fun respite from her usual editorial work on nine-hundred-page historical nonfiction tomes about the history of Manchuria or whatever. I'm very grateful to Allison Adler, who initially saw the potential in this book and went to the mat for it, and to Emma Allen at the *New Yorker* for her support of these letters long before the idea of a book had occurred to me. Also Jason Richman of the United Talent Agency and Johnny Pariseau (formerly thereof), for helping me cross over into this community and for being my kindred spirits in loving the highbrow and lowbrow equally, i.e., understanding that the best place to talk about who's getting the Booker Prize is a garbage dive bar.

I can't thank my family enough for being so supportive and brilliant, specifically Margaret, Barry, Juliana, Megan

Fogel, and Cappy Fogel. Dad, that Oxford comma was for you.

And last but not least, there's my de facto family—my community of close friends who were always there to read drafts and talk me through the writing process during meditative walks around various reservoirs, over midnight snacks at over-lit frozen yogurt franchises, and in epic phone marathons while one or both of us sat in Los Angeles traffic. They are, in alphabetical order: Taryn Aronson, Ginny Fleming, Jared Frieder, Julie Fulton, Amy Funkenstein, Meredith Goldstein, Maryhope Howland, Elinor Hutton, David Iserson, Julia Jones, Aditi Khorana, Jordana Mollick, Abdi Nazemian, Daria Polatin, Jaime Reichner, Margaret Riley, Julia Ruchman, Larry Salz, Nona Schamus, Stacey Vanek Smith, and Dahvi Waller.

One of those people is actually my therapist. I'd like her to know how much I appreciate her too.

About the Author

SUSANNA FOGEL is a Rhode Island native and apologist. She writes and directs films and television, including the comedy feature *Life Partners* and the ABC television series *Chasing Life*. She is an alumna of the Sundance Screenwriters Lab and Columbia University. Her writing has appeared in *The New Yorker* and *Time* magazine. She lives in New York and Los Angeles. And she has bangs, obviously.